Under a Bloody Flag
Book one
War in the West Series

ISBN: 978-0-9845926-6-1
Library of Congress Control Number: 2010918348
Published by Global Authors Publications

Filling the GAP in publishing

Edited by Barbara Sachs Sloan
Interior Design by KathleenWalls
Cover Design by Kathleen Walls
Cover Art: John Steuart Curry's *Tragic Prelude,*
a mural in the Kansas Statehouse
illustrating John Brown and the clash of forces in Bleeding Kansas
used courtesy of Kansas State Historical Society

Printed in USA for Global Authors Publications

Under a Bloody Flag

Book one

War in the West Series

Kathleen Walls

Dedication:

To the memory of my mother and father,
Mary Rita Shereck Reugger (12/18/1909--12/26/1989)
and Robert Joseph Reugger (3/1/1906--5/11/1985).

My mother first kindled my interest in history and my own ancestors
however my father had the ancestor with the most interesting history.

Naturally, without them this book would not exist.

Acknowledgment:

A big thank you to two people who helped critique this book: Renée Gordon and Lydia Filzen, AKA, Lydia Hawke. Lydia, who writes about the War Between the States, offered help with period-correct phrasing and helped make the novel flow better. Renée, who is a fellow travel writer, history buff and staff-writer for the *Philadelphia Sunday Sun*, offered valuable insight into African-American history and viewpoints.

Another person who has made this book even better is my editor, friend and fellow author, Barbara Sachs Sloan. She is the one who refuses to allow my misspellings and grammatical errors to slip through and often catches embarrassing mistakes before they end up in print.

A very special thank you goes out to the Kansas and Missouri Convention and Visitors Bureaus' representatives who introduced me to Freedom's Frontier National Heritage Trail: Judy Billings, Lawrence Convention & Visitors Bureau Director and Executive Director, Freedom's Frontier National Heritage Area, Debbie White, Manager, Lawrence Visitor Information Center and Susan Henderson, Marketing Director, Lawrence Convention & Visitors Bureau. You planted the idea in my head for this book series and it would not leave me alone until I wrote them. There were so many inspirational events on that trip.

I want to thank Paul Bahnmaier, Lecompton Historical Society and the Le-compton Players for an interesting look at civics in action in the 19th century. Kerry Altenbernd, whose reenactment of John Brown at Blackjack Battlefield gave me a new insight into a well-known character; and Carol Bohl, Executive Director Cass County Historical Society, who shed new light on the background of Cole Younger and William Quantrill as she portrayed Bursheba Younger at the Sharp-Hopper Cabin in Harrisonville, MO.

The number of web sites on anything related to Kansas and Missouri have been a wonderful resource. I have visited thousands so cannot mention all but if you have a site related to this era, thank you as I have probably been there and gleaned one or more tidbits of information from you.

Again the number of books I read related to this time period is enormous, too many to list here. Some were just for the feeling of the period; others offered valuable information. *Three Years With Quantrill: A True Story Told by His Scout John McCorkle*; *The Devil Knows How To Ride: The True Story Of William Clarke Quantril And His Confederate Raiders* by Edward E. Leslie; *I, Quantrill* by Max McCoy; *Bloody Bill Anderson: The Short, Savage Life of a Civil War Guerrilla* by Albert E. Castel and Thomas Goodrich; *Tragic Prelude: Bleeding Kansas* by Karen Zeinert; *The Story of Cole Younger, by Himself* by Cole Younger; *Jim Lane: Scoundrel, Statesman, Kansan* by Robert Collins and the e-book *Collections of the Kansas State Historical Society* were particularly helpful. To all I mentioned and any I may have missed, I offer heartfelt thanks.

Foreword

This is a work of fiction. My main characters and many of the minor ones are fictional. These people are totally the invention of my own mind and are modeled on types of people who settled Kansas Territory. Since there was tremendous variety among the settlers, my characters are likewise varied. As many as possible are real historical personages. Since I wasn't there when they spoke, their conversations are created based on their own personal history. Letters, books, diaries and other records of the time furnished a basis for who these people were and what they believed.

Because of the vernacular of the times, I have used many racial words that I, and I am sure my readers, find repugnant. However, to remain true to the era and the personalities of my characters, these words must be used. Many of these characters would not use any other terms. That was a part of those times.

Settlers to Kansas Territory fell into three groups with most people ranging in between either extreme. Some migrated from northern states only to be sure Kansas entered the union as a free state. Opposing settlers poured in mainly from Missouri and other southern states to be sure Kansas became a slave state. The vast majority came because it was an opportunity to get cheap land and make a living. They were prepared for hard work, hardship and long hours. They were not prepared for the bloodshed and violence that was forced upon them by extremists of both camps.

This book and its sequel, *Under a Black Flag* which will follow my same characters into the bloody war that followed, are not about who was right or wrong. It is about human beings, most a mixture of good and bad, Black, white and Indian, who tried to live out their lives as they chose on America's most deadly frontier.

Under a Bloody Flag

In Kansas and Missouri, the War Between the States started long before Fort Sumter. Daniel Fitzgerald, a Southerner who tries to settle Kansas and leave behind his tormented Louisiana roots, soon finds that in Kansas Territory you have to take sides or die. Taking sides doesn't lessen the chances of a violent death, it just determines who is going to try and kill you.

For Massachusetts-born Rebecca Styles, who comes to Kansas to insure freedom for slaves, the choice is easy. Or is it? When she meets Daniel, she is forced to take a new look at all the ideas she took for granted, like all Southerners are evil and all abolitionists are good.

Daniel's half-brother and former slave, André, knows his first loyalty belongs to his friends and family, not a lofty ideal, but he can't sit by and do nothing when injustice stares him in the face.

Throw into the mix all the larger-than-life characters who played a part in the sectional violence which led the nation into its bloodiest war and you have a novel with all the drama of the era. You'll meet James Lane, John Brown, JEB Stuart, Robert E. Lee, Joseph Shelby, Harriet Tubman, Abraham Lincoln, and the other men and women who have shaped this nation into what it is today.

You will never look at any of them as just characters in a history book again.

This is a historical novel unlike any you have ever read before. It is a blend of history, action and romance. Facts read like fiction, and fiction could have been fact. It is a story of a time that changed a nation and a handful of people who lived and died in our nation's most colorful era.

"If civil war is to be the result, in such a conflict there cannot be and will not be any neutrals recognized. 'He that is not for us is against us' will of necessity be the motto; and those who are not willing to take either one side or the other are the most unfortunate men in Kansas, and had better flee to other regions as expeditiously as possible - they are not the men for Kansas." Article in the *Squatter Sovereign*, June 5, 1856. J. H. Stringfellow, editor.

 Prologue

April 10, 1856—Saint Bernard Parish, Louisiana

The bright Louisiana sun streaming through the open French windows illuminated the rich brocade of the drapes and the gleaming mahogany of the bedroom furnishings. The rich smell of coffee and chicory emanated from the silver pot on the night table. It appeared to be just another day at Irish Luck Plantation. The fact did not permeate to the upper reaches of the home that the dead mistress of the plantation lay in state downstairs, surrounded by the few guests who had remained at the side of the coffin for a traditional wake. However, the dead woman, Colette Bordelon Fitzgerald, was the focus of each of the three persons in the magnificent upstairs room.

Daniel's face was flushed and his hands clutched as if to grasp the handle of a sword. "Sir, you insulted my mother while she lived, and now your words shame her after death. If you were not my father, I would call you out! Damn, I will call you out even so. From now on you are no father of mine."

Michael Fitzgerald motioned to the frightened slave woman. "Return to the kitchen, Elise." He turned to his son as the woman scurried out the bedroom door. "Daniel, you do not understand." Only the unnatural pallor of his face betrayed the anger the big Irishman was successfully holding back.

"Oh, I understand," Daniel replied. "You are consoling yourself with a slave woman while my mother lies in her coffin downstairs. You are contemptible. You…"

"No! It's you, whelp, that dinna understand." The brogue Michael had learned to repress returned in times of stress.

1

"My mother is dead and you begin raping Elise, who has no choice in the matter. Oh, I understand only..."

"No. Listen for once. You may be my son, but you go too far. No man insults me as you do and lives. I worked too hard to build this plantation and make the Fitzgerald name one to command respect in this Frenchie dominated Louisiana. *I* am the reason you have had the best tutors and dress like a gentleman. Yes, *I* am the reason you are idle by day and prance around saloons and cat houses by night. You owe me everything. *Me*, not your fancy French ma. You will listen."

"I will listen and then I will have my satisfaction. Father or no." Daniel's anger was worn down by his grief. To lose his beloved mother and then find his powerful father compromising himself was too hard to understand.

As the older man spoke, his words carried him back. Back to the day he had to flee Ireland to avoid the rope. Back to that cold Dec of 1831 when the Carrichshock Tithes War went so wrong. The British crushed the rebellion like all the others in the old country. Michael had been visiting from his neighboring County Kerry and had gotten caught up in fighting for the Irish right to support their own Catholic churches instead of the damned Church of England that got shoved down the starving people's throat like all the bloody English institutions and laws. He had gotten passage on the first ship to America and found himself in the port of New Orleans. He found work where he could and played cards whenever he had free time. Soon he found the cards made him a better living than the hard work. He was good at reading faces from the time in Ireland when it was hard to know who your enemy was and a mistake in judgment meant the gallows.

He bought new clothes which allowed him entrance to the pricier saloons and brothels where the rich planters idled away their free time. The same places his son took for granted as a form of amusement. Michael never saw them as a pastime. For Michael, they were places where he earned a living. His lifestyle got even better the night he played Bourré with Jacques Bordelon and a few friends. Jacques was convinced he was the world's greatest player of the old Cajun card game, but this night he was losing badly to Michael. He was well into his cups as well, so when Michael had cleared the chips from the table and all the other players had called it a night and politely acknowledged Michael as the night's undisputed winner, Jacques would not leave it be. He insisted on a "winner take all" single hand of poker. Just the two of them. Jacques was out of cash, but he put up the deed to his plantation in Saint Bernard Parish near Meraux, Louisiana.

The hand went quickly. Michael held two kings and drew a third.

Jacques ended with only a pair of tens. Like the gentleman he was raised to be, Jacques dutifully signed over the deed to Michael. Sheriff Louis Meraux and another man witnessed it, and the deed was done. Michael now owned a plantation. Jacques retired to an upstairs room with one of the "ladies," Suziee, asked her to leave him for a moment, then blew out his brains all over the narrow bed. Suziee was far more upset than Michael.

When he surveyed his new domain the next morning, Michael was quite upset."What have I gotten myself into here?"

Jacques had forgotten to mention the place was infested with marsh rats; the fields which should support sugar cane and rice were mostly stubble. He was disappointed when he entered the sagging-roofed, once-white home that stood at the end of an oak-lined drive. He found only one slave within, a mulatto woman named Elise. An even worse shock awaited him in one of the upstairs bedrooms. There he confronted a weeping girl, who, he finally understood from conversation between the tears and sobs, was Jacques' sixteen-year-old daughter, Colette.

"I did the honorable thing when I married your mother. I renamed the plantation Irish Luck and built it into one of the best sugar cane plantations in the parish." Michael continued the story. "But I never loved her. That was reserved for you when you arrived. Elise was the one I turned to for comfort, and I suppose if I were capable of loving any woman, she would be the one. Unfortunately, our different stations is life make it something I can never consider."

"All these years? What of Elise's children, André and Sallie, are they…?

"Yes," Michael snapped harshly. "I sired them. Are you satisfied now?"

"Satisfied?" Daniel retorted. "André, my body servant, my friend, my brother?"

Daniel could bear no more. He swung a strong right fist toward his father's chin. Michael had not lost his fighter's instincts after all these years. He deflected the blow and placed one of his own on his son's unguarded right eye. "No man strikes me and goes unpunished. You are lucky you are my son or…"

"I am my mother's son." Daniel spun away from his father and headed for the door. He pushed past all the funeral guests in his haste to be out of this house that now held only hatred and repulsion for him. "You are no longer my father, this is not my home, it is Hell. I will never set foot here again. And you. I cannot find it in myself to kill you, but never call me 'son' again."

 Chapter 1

May 24, 1856—Kansas Territory

Dan sat on the banks of the creek. The night was warm and muggy. The moon was full enough to see his trotline corks bobbing in the water and his damp clothes resting on the bank next to him. It shed enough light to see André splashing in the deeper part of the creek. The line of cottonwood trees hid the small log cabin the two of them had thrown up so hurriedly in the past two weeks since they had arrived in Kansas Territory. The cabin was just a temporary shelter until they could build something better, but getting in a crop on their forty acres was the most urgent necessity. It was all so different from Louisiana. Everything here was rough and primitive. Still he was glad to be here. So much had happened so fast since that night of his mother's funeral.

When he had left the plantation he headed for New Orleans to drink away the pain and sorrow. It was three days later in one of the sleazier cat houses when André came for him. André sobered him up and cleaned him up. It was André who made him realize he could not just drink away his life. He needed to either reconcile with his father or make his own way. Reconciling with Michael was not an option. Making his own way was a novel experience for which eighteen-year-old Daniel Kerry Fitzgerald had no familiarity. It was André who told him of the group of settlers coming from Montgomery, Alabama, by way of Mobile. Their steamship, *Florida,* had just docked in New Orleans. They were headed for Kansas Territory to support the Southern faction in making sure Kansas was admitted to the Union as a slave state. Their leader, Major Jefferson Buford, was willing to accept a few more emigrants. He offered free passage to Kansas and help for one year while the emigrants got settled on their claims.

"He's looking for 'sober, industrious young men.'" André had stated. "So we'd better get you smelling a little fresher than you do now, Danny Boy."

It had never occurred to Dan to wonder about the fact that his young servant had been allowed to sit in while Mr. Douglas, the long-suffering tutor Michael had brought in to turn his wild hellion of a son into a true Southern gentleman, had expounded good grammar along with Latin and the classics. A lot of things had never occurred to him. Like why André was so much lighter than his mother. And why Dan's own mother never seemed to have a word to say to her husband unless it related to the management of the household. Now it all made a bitter and perfect sense.

They boarded the steamer America and arrived in Kansas on May 2. Dan had lied about his age: he needed to be twenty-one to file a claim on the forty acres of Kansas land. He had in his pocket the few hundred dollars of his money and Buford's pledge of support in the new land. André had in his pocket the manumission papers making him a free man which Dan had hurriedly processed before they left New Orleans.

They had rushed from the border to claim a plot of land here on Mosquito Creek near where it flowed into the Pottawatomie Creek. It was fertile and had lots of timber, some oak and cotton wood, that was easily felled and notched to let them get the cabin, if you could call it that, standing. The cabin had four walls, not yet caulked, and a rough chimney but only a dirt floor. Although most people in Kansas Territory assumed André was a slave, Dan filed a joint claim, making his brother a full partner. They had been putting all their energy into clearing a plot of land at least big enough for a vegetable patch and a cornfield for a cash crop.

He was pulled from his reverie by the muffled but unmistakable sound of gunfire. André heard it too and was out of the water throwing on his half-dry trousers as Dan reached for his own. The two young men hurried back by way of the almost hidden trail to their cabin. The cabin was closer to reach than the horses which were penned in a rough corral on the nearby prairie land to graze. Dan had purchased two dray animals to pull the wagon and supplies he had been given based on the agreement with Major Buford. Jokingly named Trouble and Double Trouble, they were sorry specimens but better than many settlers owned. Nothing was disturbed, but there were some horse tracks and footprints in the loose dirt near the door.

"Somebody was looking for us," Dan observed. "Who would be calling after dark?"

"Could be them Free-State men," André replied. "I heard they were a bit upset by the ruckus Sheriff Sam Jones caused when he rode into Lawrence a few days ago."

"Yeah," Dan replied. "Some ruckus." He had heard all about the burning of the New England Emigrant Aid Company hotel and the destruction of two Free-State Lawrence newspapers presses. Jones' men had also burned down bogus Governor Charles Robinson's house. "At least no one was killed. It would all simmer down if they would just leave us Southerners alone. Well, let's just head down to the Doyle's cabin and make sure they are all right."

Before they reached their neighbor's cabin, they made a gruesome discovery. What appeared to be a dead body lay on the side of the road. Dan saw blood still flowing from the numerous slashes on the wounded man's hands and arm. "My God! It's Drury Doyle." He tried to staunch the bleeding and brushed away some of the blood from the head.

Even in the moonlight, they could tell it was too late to help Drury. He was bleeding profusely from large cuts all over, and it was clear he was beyond help. Drury recognized his new friend, Dan, and tried to tell him what had happened. "Ol' John Brown. He came to our cabin. There was eight of them. Took me and Willie and Dad. Shot Dad and cut Willie to pieces. I tried to escape. They caught me, slashed me with their swords." The boy sank into a stupor, then seemed to find a last spurt of strength. "They went to your cabin first. Guess you weren't there. Goin' to Wilkinson's now. Help us. Help Mom and Polly and the little uns." Drury slumped once again. This time his life had flowed away.

Stunned, Dan laid Drury on the side of the path, and André covered the boy's face with his kerchief. "He was only twenty years old," Dan murmured.

"Let's get up to the cabin and see if he was right about Mr. James and Willie," André said.

Just about 200 yards from the Doyle cabin, they made the second gory find. James Doyle and his son, William, lay dead a few inches apart. James had been shot in the head and hacked by broadswords until his arm was almost severed. William had suffered the same hacking death as his brother. Dan spotted William's detached hand and had to look away from the sickening sight. "Whoever did this is long gone now. Mrs. Doyle and the children should be safe enough for the moment. Let's see if we can get to Wilkinson's place in time." Dan said. "There's a short cut through the woods."

Allen Wilkinson, a member of the Kansas Legislature, was their next nearest neighbor. His wife, Louisa Jane, had been sick with the measles. Their children were all younger than Dan, so he didn't know them as well as he had known Drury and William Doyle who were just a few years older than him. The Doyle boys, their father and younger brother, John, had helped put up the small cabin Dan and André shared. They had hunted and shared meals together. Best of all they had accepted André as part of the crowd. *How could someone kill another human being just because they came from a different part of the county, had different belief?* Dan thought. *This can't be happening.*

When they reached the Wilkinson cabin, Dan saw it *had* happened again. Allen Wilkinson lay just about a hundred fifty yards from his cabin. He had been hacked to death and his skull split open.

Dan was debating whether to go to the cabin and attempt to comfort Mrs. Wilkinson or try and guess where the marauders might strike next when hoofbeats alerted him. As one, he and André ducked into the nearby brush.

It seemed like forever before the group of men on horseback had passed. It was that darkest hour just before dawn, so they could not make out any faces. "I think that must have been the murderers." Dan was afraid even now to raise his voice above a whisper.

"Yeah," replied André. "They sure seemed happy, hooting and hollering like that."

The two young men tried to track the horsemen but soon realized it was useless. "Besides," Dan reasoned, "they must have been headed back home or they would not have been making so much racket."

They doubled back to the Wilkinsons' cabin intending to speak to Mrs. Wilkinson and offer what help they could before returning to the Doyles' to do the same for Mrs. Doyle. As they arrived near the cabin, once again they heard horses and men approaching. They ducked into the bushes near the body. By now it was full daylight, and the bushes did not offer much concealment.

As the second riders reached the clearing around the Wilkinson cabin, André whispered to Dan, "It's Mr. Harris. He has a claim not too far from here. Wonder who that lady riding with him is?"

When Dan hailed him, James Harris seemed glad to see that it was Dan and André. He and the lady dismounted, and Harris handed the reins to André to tend. Mr. Harris explained what had happened after the killers left the Wilkinson house. "William Sherman and some others were staying overnight at my house. A short time ago, Old Captain John Brown and seven other men came there, and after taking some property, they questioned me and others. Then Old Brown asked Sherman to go out with him, and he did. I heard nothing more for about fifteen minutes. Two of the 'Northern Army,' as they styled themselves, stayed with us until they heard a cap burst, and then these two men left. At first light I started looking, and I found William Sherman dead, in the creek near my house. I took his body out of the creek and examined it. Sherman's skull was split open in two places, and some of his brains were washed out by the water; a large hole was cut in his breast, and his left hand was cut off, except a little piece of skin on one side. I'm telling you, boy, the devil is about this night."

"After seeing this, I have a feeling the devil is going to trouble us for a lot longer than one night," Dan replied.

The lady with Harris coughed gently. He seemed to have forgotten

7

her presence in the excitement. "Oh, sorry. All this has driven off all my manners. Daniel, this is Mrs. Whiteman. She was visiting at our cabin, and I could not leave her there to fend for herself."

Mrs. Whiteman went to the cabin to tell Mrs. Wilkinson the sad news and provide what comfort she could. Harris decided to accompany her, and Dan and André proceeded to the Doyles' cabin to offer what help they could. Harris and Dan agreed to organize a meeting of all the settlers around the area for the following day. Harris planned to notify the sheriff after he spoke to Mrs. Wilkinson.

The front yard of the Doyle cabin was bedlam. Mahala Doyle stood sobbing hysterically over the bodies of her husband and William. John, the sixteen-year-old son, tried to comfort his mother while he kept brushing his own hand over his eyes surreptitiously. Little Polly Ann tried to calm her shrieking younger brothers, ten-year-old James, eight-year-old Charles and five-year-old Henry.

John appeared pathetically relieved to see someone he perceived as the voice of authority even if it was only a neighbor a few years older than himself. "Danny, Ma's out of her mind with the sorrow of it. I dinna know what to do. Da's dead and Willie and Drury. What's going to happen to us?"

Dan shook the younger boy's hand and offered a rough masculine hug. "I'll talk to your ma, John. Don't know if it will help any." He approached Mrs. Doyle. "I'm so sorry for your loss, ma'am." He didn't mention that Drury had lived long enough to tell him some of what happened. Better for her to think he died quickly. The slashes denied any possibility of an easy death.

"Jim was a good man. He just done what he had ta do to take care of his family. He might'a yelled at some of them Free-Staters, but he never killed no one. We had ta join the Pro-Slavery Law and Order Party. No un'll let a body stay neutral in Kansas." She glanced over at André. "We never owned slaves. Never could'a afforded any nor wanted any no how. Why?"

"Miz Doyle, I promise you I will do all I can to make those men pay for what they did."

"I do thank you for that. But it won't bring 'em back. The black-hearted devil even killed Jim's dog, Ol' Patch. She had a pair of pups, but he must'a killed them too. We buried the dog over there near where we're fixin' to bury Jim and the boys. She was starting to attract buzzards. John can build some coffins from wood that Jim had cut for a barn. I'd like fer you to say a few words along with some of the other folks around here. He was so impressed by you and felt you would do well in Kansas. He had gotten mighty fond of André as well. My Jim was well liked by folks 'round here and deserves a decent wake." Her sweeping hand gesture indicated a small cleared plot of land on a slight slope where wildflowers still bloomed just past the cleared patch.

"André and I will help John with the coffins this afternoon. We're meeting tomorrow after all the burying to decide what we can do. Mr. Harris is riding over to Sheriff Jones to let him know about these killings."

Something in his face must have let her know there was more about the night she didn't know. "There were others killed?"

"Yes, ma'am. After they finished with Drury, they went to Wilkinsons' and Harrises' cabins. Killed Mr. Wilkinson and Mr. Sherman at the Harris place."

"Kansas Territory ain't safe for me and mine no more. I'm giving up my claim. Jim and me, we worked this claim since November last year. Just wanted to make a home for us and the young uns. You can have it if you want it."

"Ma'am, I'll help if you want to stay. André and I will do whatever we can to help."

"You're a good boy, Danny, and you've been a good neighbor the few weeks you been here. No, I'll not stay here a day more than it takes ta bury me dead. Then it's back to Missouri or maybe our old place in Chattanooga, Tennessee. Only there ain't nothing there for us now. Po' whites like us cain't make a livin' in a slave state."

"Thank you, Miz Doyle. I have a few dollars left out of my savings and I want to pay you something for the claim."

"I'd appreciate any money you could spare to buy the claim. We ain't got much savings. I'll get work and take care of the young uns somehow."

Young John had approached in time to hear the last part of the conversation. He added, "Don't you worry none, Ma, I'll find work and help out. Sure will miss Willy and Druey. And Pa."

Both of the older Doyles looked like they were about to break out in a fresh outburst of tears. The younger ones had never stopped sniffling. Dan offered the only comfort he could. "I can promise I will keep the gravesites cleared and tidy." He knew it was cold comfort at best, but it was all he had to offer at the moment. He thought of one other thing that almost went without saying. "It looks like a war has broken loose, but I won't forget Mr. Doyle or the boys. I'll do everything in my power to avenge them. I give you my solemn promise as long as I stand on this Kansas soil, I will hunt down and kill those who did such a cruel thing."

At the meeting of the local settlers held the next day, Dan got his first taste of bureaucratic maneuvering. Naturally, all agreed to band together to protect one another. It was generally decided Captain Henry

Clay Pate, the Kansas correspondent for the *Missouri Republican*, who headed the militia of the Law and Order Party, The Westport Sharpshooters, could be counted on to capture Old Brown and bring him and his men to justice. Pate was also appointed a deputy United States Marshal with power to arrest.

Dan signed up for the militia, and Captain Pate told him to get his affairs in order and meet at their camp in three days. Meantime, he decided to take matters into his own hands and go to Lawrence and do a little spying.

"It's only for a few days, André. I'll be back before you know I'm gone."

"Don't see why I can't go with you," André insisted.

"Don't be crazy. You're a Negro and this is Lawrence we're talking about, the Free Staters' haven. Jayhawker Heaven."

"So what? I'm a free Negro even though no one seems to realize it here," André replied logically.

"They won't in Lawrence either. You'll just attract attention. I plan on riding in quietly, gathering information and returning back home again. Nothing to it. I'll just get the information and cut dirt."

Lawrence had a raw new look to it. It also had the look of a prim New England town. The burned hulk of the Free State Hotel was the only incongruous note. Nothing like the lush softness of New Orleans. Dan left Double Trouble at the livery stable and walked toward the river. *The Whitney House. Since the Free State Hotel was burned down in the raid, it's as good a place as any to start.*

When he entered the lobby, luck was on his side. No one was behind the counter. *I can sneak a peek at the register, and no one will be the wiser..*

He quickly stepped behind the counter, keeping one eye on the door to the left behind it. He was thumbing through the register for the past few days when he heard the unmistakable click of a gun's hammer. Dan looked over the counter and found himself staring down the barrel of a Colt Navy Revolver. It looked dangerous. But not half as dangerous as the person who held it leveled at his head. Some women just looked deadly in black.

Chapter 2

May 27, 1856—Lawrence, Kansas Territory

Rebecca Styles never expected to catch a robber when she offered to mind the Whitney House reception desk for her friend, Lydia Stone, while she accompanied her father, Nathan, to the dentist. But here Rebecca was, alone in the hotel lobby holding Nathan's gun on a stranger.

True, he didn't look like the average thief. In fact, he was very good looking and dressed like a gentleman in a double-breasted gray frock coat, cream-colored linen shirt and well-fitted charcoal trousers. His wavy brown hair had glints of sun in it. His complexion confirmed him to be a man who spent a lot of time outdoors. His eyes, the deepest brown she had ever seen, were locked on her own green ones.

She brushed back a strand of red-gold hair which had escaped from the scrimshaw combs she wore in an attempt to tame her unruly locks. He was quite a few inches taller than her and although slim, he looked muscular enough to easily overpower her if he wished.

She tried to hold the gun firmer in her trembling hands. "Sir, what are you doing here?"

"It's perfectly innocent. I can explain if you'll put the gun down, Miss," the stranger replied.

He really didn't look or talk like a criminal, but she was not taking any chances. His accent was too Southern. She kept the gun pointed at him. "You sound like a Georgia slaver come to do more damage to our God-fearing town. Do you plan to burn down the Whitney House like you and your Border Ruffians did the Free State Hotel last week?"

"No, ma'am. I had nothing to do with the sheriff's raid on Lawrence. And, no, I'm not from Georgia, and I do not own any slaves."

His smile would have definitely melted ice, but he *was* a Southerner and all of them were treacherous scoundrels. Her late father had warned her about slippery Southerners before they came out here last year. Her gun never wavered. "What's your name and why are you sneaking behind the counter?"

"I'm so sorry. I totally forgot my manners. Your gun makes me a little nervous. I'm Daniel Kerry Fitzgerald, at your service, and I was looking to see if a friend had arrived and already registered." That dazzling smile again. "Now if you would put the gun down we could talk."

"I think not, sir. I intend to hold you here until Nathan returns and let him decide what to do with you."

"I assure you, Miss whatever your name is, I mean no harm to you or the hotel or your 'God-fearing town.'"

"I'm Becky—I mean Rebecca Anne Styles."

"So nice to meet you although I would prefer we met under different circumstances. Those freckles do fit a 'Becky' so much better than a 'Rebecca Anne Styles.' May I call you Becky?"

She smiled in spite of herself. "You're not going to see enough of me to call me anything."

"Oh but that's where you're wrong. I plan on seeing an awfully lot of you." He swallowed hard. "Unmm, I mean I plan on *calling on you* as often as possible."

Becky felt the blush coming but could do nothing to avoid it. The curse of having fair skin. She couldn't help visualizing him *seeing more* of her. Perhaps in a sleek low-cut ball gown instead of this ugly black dress she wore in mourning for her father. She caught herself. *Oh, Becky what are you thinking. You have been reading too many of those cheap novels instead of your Bible like a good girl should.*

The arrival of Nathan and Lydia prevented Becky's thoughts from going any further. Nathan was holding a wet bandana like a compress on an obviously swollen lower jaw. "Oh, Nathan," Becky exclaimed, "I caught this man rifling through the record book behind the counter. I had stepped out to take care of some necessary, um, functions, you know." She felt another blush coming on.

"You did right, Becky. Now perhaps you might hand me the gun before it goes off and makes a worse mess than the dang dentist made of my jaws." He laid the compress aside to hold the gun with both hands.

Nathan studied Dan more closely. "You don't look like the average Border Ruffian, sir. Most of them drift in from Missouri and are unkempt and unshaven."

Rebecca and Lydia stood to the side while Nathan finished questioning the "Ruffian."

Although Becky tried to give the stranger the benefit of the doubt, she could see his story did not hold up. Dan's obviously fictitious alibi along with his Southern accent seemed to convince Nathan the man was at least involved with the Pro-Slavers. Becky realized it created a problem as to how to deal with the intruder. Since the county sheriff, Samuel Jones, was responsible for the sacking of the town a short time ago, they obviously could not turn over the prisoner to him. Nathan half-heartedly suggested calling together a few loyal men and stringing him up, but Lydia and Becky were horrified.

"He deserves a fair trial," Becky insisted.

So Nathan and Becky marched Dan upstairs to one of the unoccupied rooms and locked him in until someone in authority could be consulted.

As they headed downstairs, Nathan confided to Becky, "I'll call in Colonel Lane and turn Mr. Fitzgerald over to him."

"Colonel Lane," Becky sniffed, "is not a gentleman, Nathan. I dare not stand near him at a gathering. He actually attempts to touch me in very inappropriate places. He says things which could be construed improperly, too. And all the while his wife is sitting across the room."

"Colonel Lane has a reputation, but if he bothers you again tell me and I will confront him. Since your father died last year, you know you can count on me to protect you. I feel like you are my daughter just like Lydia. You girls have been so close since we all came out here. I don't trust him too far either. He was all for slavery when he first moved here from Indiana; then he changed his tune. He is an opportunist and certainly plays the field behind his wife's back. However, he is a capable military officer, though I don't want him sniffing around you or Lydia. Wouldn't trust him with my bookkeeping either."

"And you are going to turn Mr. Fitzgerald over to him?" Becky could not get those deep brown eyes out of her mind.

"Got to do something with him," Nathan retorted. "I'll send him up a dish of grub from the kitchen while he waits for the colonel."

"I'll take it up to him," Becky offered.

⌐⟋

Becky knocked before she inserted the key in the prisoner's door. "It's Rebecca Styles, Mr. Fitzgerald. I have some lunch for you."

Taking the silence to mean he was decent, Becky opened door and placed the food on a nearby table. She turned to leave, but Dan touched her gently on the arm. "Please, Miss Styles, stay and talk to me. You have my word as a gentleman I won't attempt to escape."

Becky perched on the only chair, and Dan paced the small room. "I mean no harm to you or Mr. Stone or your town. I need to find out who may have been involved in a case of cold blooded murder of some of my neighbors. We know John Brown led the raid, but who was with him and where he is now is the question."

Becky replied, "Our town co-founder Governor Robinson and Colonel Lane think highly of John Brown. In fact Mr. Robinson actually compared Mr. Brown to Jesus Christ in one of his speeches. The three confer often about the state of affairs in Kansas. Mr. Brown's heart is in the right place, but he is a bit extreme in his methods."

"If you call dragging five unarmed men, two of them not much more than boys, from their beds and hacking them to pieces in the middle of the night 'a bit extreme,' we differ on the meaning of the word."

"Oh dear God! Is that what he did?" Becky shuddered.

"Yes, it is. I will spare your feminine ears the exact details. Can you understand why I want to find him and his henchmen?" Dan replied. "And incidentally Charles Robinson is *not* the governor of Kansas territory, Wilson Shannon is. That so-called Free-State convention in Topeka was totally illegal. That's why Robinson is presently being held under arrest in Lecompton."

"Oh, why is this territory doomed to always be plagued by all this violence over politics? We came here to help make sure Kansas is not admitted as a slave state. That bogus legislature was elected by border ruffians from Missouri. That is why we passed the Topeka Constitution. Slavery is so wrong. But so is killing." Becky put her head in her hands and began to cry.

"I am inclined to agree with you on all counts," Dan replied. "However, you do realize your prized Topeka constitution excluded Negro free men from Kansas. A bit hypocritical to free Negros but not allow them into the territory."

"Oh I know. Things are in such a mess." Tears were streaming down her cheeks. He stroked her flaming hair and offered his handkerchief. "Please don't weep, Miss Styles. None of this is your fault." He leaned down to wipe her cheeks, and in an instant somehow she was leaning against his broad chest. He put his fingers under her chin and tipped hr head so their lips almost touched.

"My my, how I hate to interrupt this tender scene." A harsh male voice from the doorway brought Becky back to her senses.

She turned to face Colonel James Lane. Feeling the rush of blood to her cheeks, she knew her face was flaming. "I was overcome for a moment by some sad news, and Mr. Fitzgerald was comforting me."

"Well, how touching. Perhaps I can offer some *comfort* one day soon, Miss Styles, but for now I have a prisoner to dispose of."

Jim Lane was never a pleasant man, but with his dark hair fanning out around his gaunt sneering face and his deep set almost black eyes, Becky though he resembled pictures she had seen of the devil in her early schoolbooks. All he needed was a red cape and horns. "What are you going to do with him?"

"Well, Miss Styles, you probably don't want to know his final fate. *Most of us* around this town consider Border Ruffians only fit to decorate a fine stout oak branch. But to spare your sensibilities, for now, I have a horse with me to transport him to a proper jail until that fine day arrives."

Jim Lane roughly secured Dan's hands behind his back and led him toward the door. Something in Becky snapped. Pro-Slave or not, she could not allow Dan to hang. Almost without conscious thought, her fingers curled around the pewter pitcher of water she had brought for the prisoner's lunch. Stepping behind the colonel, she brought it down on Jim Lane's head with all of her strength. He crumpled to the floor, and Becky wasted only a passing thought as to whether she might have killed the man before turned her attention to Dan. She cut the rope binding his hands with a small knife she had brought with the food. "I couldn't let Colonel Lane hang you." She shrugged as if knocking out colonels was an everyday occurrence. "Follow me."

With no better option, Dan bent and kissed the hand of his deliverer. "I am completely at your service and deeply in your debt, Miss Becky."

Becky brought Dan to Nathan and his wife's room next door and picked up a bandana, duster and hat for Dan and a rubber rain slicker for herself. "Here, put these on and button up to your neck, then hold this over as much of your face as possible and follow me. Whatever you do, don't speak. We're going to walk out and mount those horses Lane said are out by the back door. I will try and get you out of town without attracting too much attention. It's pouring rain, so most people will not be about."

Becky led the way down the back stairs where two horses stood ready. One was a spirited palomino and the other a bay gelding not in the first flush of youth. If there was any question which was Lane's personal mount, the short barreled, slanted carbine, Sharp's rifle, called Beecher's Bibles in Kansas, hanging in a scabbard on his fine embossed leather saddle made it clearer. "You take the palomino. I'll ride the bay." She untied the horses. "People may notice me riding astride, but it's not unheard of out here. Sometimes we have to. If anyone gives chase, you keep going. Never mind me."

"I'll not leave you behind to face the music for rescuing me. We'll both make it out safely, or neither of us will. At least this downpour will cover our tracks quickly."

Dan helped her mount, then swung into the saddle of his new horse. As they reached the end of Massachusetts Street, Becky heard shouts and gunshots behind them. She looked back to see Jim Lane, his gun smoking and hear his powerful voice carrying over the wind and rain, "You traitorous bitch! You will live to regret this day. I'll make you pay a thousand fold."

"The race is on." Dan urged. "We have enough head start on them. We'll lose them in the woods across the river."

They easily outdistanced their pursuers, but Lane's parting words still echoed in Becky's head. She had made a powerful enemy.

15

 Chapter 3

May 27, 1856—Douglas County, Kansas Territory

Dan led Rebecca due south in the direction of Ottawa. He paralleled the California Road for a short distance, then veered off the main trace into heavier brush to elude any pursuers. The rain had finally stopped. The storm had been so heavy he doubted anyone could follow their trail. From there he planned on turning east-southeast toward Pottawatomie Creek and home. They had crossed Captains Creek when he noticed Rebecca was lagging behind and seemed to be crying. He spotted a heavily wooded place where they could rest and still be well hidden from any riders on the main trail. Slowing his horse's gait to match his companion's, he called to her, "Dismount and let's lead the horses to the creek here. They could use a drink." He took her reins along with his own and lightly looped it with a loose vine so the horses could drink but not escape. Dan and Becky shed their rain gear and pushed it into their saddlebags. "You look like you have a problem."

Rebecca looked at him through her tears. "'A problem' the man says? Why, yes, Mr. Fitzgerald, I *do* have a problem. In good conscience, I could not let you be hanged by Colonel Lane. So without anymore thought, I struck him, knocked him unconscious and helped a criminal escape."

"So you did. However, I don't see myself as a criminal. I am eternally grateful."

"Oh, you huge lummox, can't you see where my impulsive actions have placed me? I can never go back to Lawrence." Becky began to sob in earnest now.

A woman's tears always unnerved Dan. He was never sure whether to run away and let her cry in private or reach out and give her a comforting pat on the back. In Becky's case, he wanted to enfold her in his arms and offer her a different kind of comfort. He reached out toward her and then pulled his hand back. Rebecca Styles was not the kind of young woman with whom he usually consorted. That brand of comfort would not do for a gently-bred lady at all. Even if she was a damned New England abolitionist. *Especially* since she was a New England abolitionist. He reluctantly put his hands in his pockets when a few strands of gorgeous flaming hair worked loose from the pair of delicate ivory colored combs she used to pin it back. He had to fight the temptation to touch to see if it felt as soft as it looked. "I can help you return wherever you want to go. Do you have family back in New England?"

She began to cry even harder.

Way to go, Fitzgerald. Tact was never your strong suit. "Is there someone special back in Lawrence? I could say it was me who hit Lane and then forced you to come with me." He dug in his pocket for a bandana and handed the faded red square to her. "Here, dry those pretty eyes. I'll even write a note clearing you."

She managed to laugh and cry at the same time. "I don't think it's quite so simple. Lane had you in clear view all the time. And no, I have no family in New England. No family anywhere since my father died last year."

"Oh. I'm sorry to hear that. Are there friends anywhere you could go to?"

"No," she repeated. "There is no one anywhere except the Stones."

The sadness in her eyes was more than he could bear. A new solution presented itself. Too ridiculous to consider yet he was considering it. "I have another idea. Hear me out before you reply."

She blinked back her tears. "What?"

"It may sound a little strange considering we only met this morning."

"This entire day has been strange. What do you have in mind?'

"We could get married."

"Married?" She looked at him as if he had gone mad.

Indeed he felt as if he had gone mad. What gentleman proposes to a young lady after less than a day's acquaintance? However, what gentleman finds himself in such a predicament? He owed her his life, yet she was a total stranger. His father's story about the winning of Irish Luck and subsequent marriage to Collette Bordelon crept unbidden into his thoughts. At least he was attracted to Rebecca.

"It seems a logical way to handle things. After all we are both unmarried and somewhat adrift out here on the frontier and …"

"Logical?" Becky's laughter had a tinge of hysteria to it. "Exactly what every Massachusetts girl dreams of, a 'logical' proposal from a slave owner."

Dan's feelings prickled a little at her reaction. Plenty of Louisiana girls would have jumped at the chance to wed Daniel Kerry Fitzgerald. "I'm not a slave owner! André is a free man. And this is the only way I see to make it possible for you to live in my cabin. Naturally, I'm a gentleman and would not make any indecent advances until... I mean

17

unless you consent. After all, many people marry without ever meeting. Where I come from marriages are often arranged when children of neighboring plantations are very young. Society is not kind to a spinster, and a man needs… well, marriage is a social commitment as well as a romantic one." He was floundering, and he knew it. *Shut up, Fitzgerald. Anything you say will only make thing worse.*

She stopped laughing and reached out her hand. The first time she had voluntarily touched him since they left the hotel. He felt the sparks and knew she did as well. "Please, Mr. Fitzgerald, I'm not laughing at you. I only meant to say our backgrounds are diametrically opposed and we don't know the first thing about one another."

He realized he really wanted this marriage to take place. Not only to save her reputation. He wanted this woman as he had never wanted another. They had met under difficult circumstances. Yet a spark was there, and it had never been there for any other woman. "We do know some things. I know you are a tender-hearted woman who believes in doing the right thing no matter the personal cost. And you must know I am a man of principle. It may not be much, but it is a start." He hesitated unused to stating his most intimate feelings. "And surely you are aware I find you attractive and have reason to believe you do not find me repulsive."

Becky blushed. "You are certainly a gentleman, and I do not find you repulsive."

"Then you will consider my proposal?"

She stared at him, and he sensed the turmoil in play behind her lovely blue eyes. Finally, she murmured, "I don't have too many other opportunities, do I?"

Dan hated the feeling that she considered his offer her only option. "I will try and be a good husband to you. I am not doing this out of duty only. I think you will be a wonderful wife."

"We don't really know each other," she repeated. "I always expected to get to know my future husband well before we... I mean, Mr. Fitzgerald, I will be honored to become your wife." The blush deepened. "However, I will need some time to become accustomed… I mean, to allow personal liberties between us."

He took her hand and replied. "As long as you need." Inwardly, he grimaced. *Fitzgerald, you have really let yourself in for it now. How long can you live in close quarters with this attractive woman and not take things to their natural conclusion?*

Dan and Rebecca arrived at the small cabin well after midnight.

This Negro man Daniel had mentioned, André, was nowhere in sight. They shared a few stale biscuits, an apple and a bit of venison jerky Daniel found wrapped in a piece of cloth on the stump they currently used as a table. Rebecca didn't voice a complaint; however, she could not help thinking this was the poorest cabin she had ever seen.

Daniel must have seen her disappointment. "The big push was to get a corn crop in the ground and make this a profitable venture. As soon as I get back from riding with Captain Pate to find those murderers who killed the Doyles and the others, I'll build you a fine necessary behind the house," he promised. "André and I have been using the woods. I know that is more difficult for a lady."

"I'll be fine," Rebecca replied. "For now, is there a private spot nearby, and may I take this lantern?"

"Of course. Go around near the back corner. Is there anything else you umm … need for now?" Becky was surprised to see Daniel blushing.

"Just a little water to wash the worst of the trail dirt away." She picked up the flickering lantern, scooped a dipperful of water from the full bucket near the door into a smaller bucket sitting next to it and stepped out among the low-hanging willows and tall cottonwood trees.

When she returned, Daniel was admiring Lane's rifle. "A fine piece of workmanship. Very accurate. Much easier to load on horseback." He laid it next to one of the two sets of woolen blankets arranged in opposite corners of the room. "I guess André may have gone out hunting and you'll meet him in the morning. Now that our corn crop is in the ground I can concentrate on fixing up the cabin." Dan gazed around the shabby interior. "I'll also put in a more permanent kitchen as soon as I can."

Rebecca removed her shoes and her grandfather's combs and tried to get comfortable curled up in the rough blankets. She heard Daniel saying something about "getting a preacher to marry them as soon as possible." And she drifted off into a troubled sleep. Her last thought was *What have I gotten myself into? I haven't chosen an easy life, but Daniel seems like a good man.*

The door burst open, silhouetting a tall, dark figure holding a rifle in the dim moonlight, and a rough voice shouted, "Don't make a false move or I'll blow you to Kingdom Come!"

Rebecca bolted upright and screamed. Daniel stumbled to his feet and grabbed her, pushing her behind his body. "We have no guns. Don't shoot."

The figure stepped into the room and reached for the lantern. "Is that you, Danny Boy?" He struck a lucifer and lit the lantern wick. "Oh hellfire, I thought you were some of those damned abolitionists."

Daniel stepped aside, revealing Becky. "Good morning or night, whichever it is, André. May I present Miss Rebecca Styles, my fiancée?"

The tall man lowered the gun. He nudged the Sharp's with his boot toe. "No guns, huh?"

Dan shrugged as if to say, "People who burst in on someone in the middle of the night deserve to be lied to."

Rebecca observed a light-complexioned Negro man, a few years older than Daniel and, like Daniel, slim and well muscled. He now seemed as much at a loss for words as he had been in command of the situation a few moments ago. "Your fiancée? Begging your pardon, ma'am, for my language a few moments ago. I saw two strange horses outside, and with Old John Brown and his bunch of abolitionists still roaming the territory, I thought... well I don't know what I thought." He looked at Daniel. "I sure didn't expect you to bring back a 'fiancée' from Lawrence."

Daniel replied, "Actually it is more like she brought me back. If it hadn't been for her intervention, I'd be a cottonwood blossom by now." He explained the happenings in Lawrence.

"Don't I remember you saying 'nothing to it'? I'll get the information and cut dirt back. Don't need any help.' Must have misheard you." André's lips curled in a mocking grin.

Daniel ignored the jibe. "Reckon it's time to get an early start on the day. I need to ride into Westport and join up with Pate's militia tomorrow. They plan to start out hunting Old Brown and his murdering cronies. I'd be much obliged if you would quit grinning like a scalded 'possum and ride into Lane City and see if you can find us a clergyman willing to marry us while I at least make a start on a real necessary."

He turned to Rebecca. "I am a Catholic but will be happy to locate any clergyman to perform the ceremony. Do you have any strong feelings on the subject?"

"I might have guessed you're a Papist as well as a slave—" She cast a quick glance in André's direction, *Former* slave owner. No, any denomination will do. I am...was a member of the Congregational Church in Lawrence. I guess that is of no importance anymore."

André looked from Rebecca to Daniel. Becky could see understanding dawning in his eyes. "Lawrence? You mean she is a dam... I mean an abolitionist?"

"Reckon so." Daniel shrugged. "As the lady says, it makes no difference anymore."

"Well, it might make a tad of difference to a few of the more radical elements around these parts. Moving on to less sticky subjects, Mrs. Doyle left yesterday while you were hobnobbing around Lawrence with your fiancée. She said you had been good to her and her boys and had given her some money, so she signed a paper deeding you her claim. It's probably about as legal as the bogus legislature in Pawnee. However, the way things are going I guess that's of no importance either. Leastwise, the lady will have more comfortable lodgings than our little *garçonnière.*"

"Wonderful!" Realizing what he said, Daniel clarified. "For us I mean, not for poor Mrs. Doyle. I never believed she would leave this soon."

"She says she is afraid to stay any longer with Old Brown on the loose." André glanced in Becky's direction. "She believed he may come back after young John,"

Rebecca was totally confused until Daniel explained about his arrangement with Mrs. Doyle. He added, "The cabin has a nice necessary and a fine outdoor kitchen as well as a good fireplace inside for cooking in inclement weather. It will be a better home for you once we are married."

André offered a mock bow. "Massa, I's goin' to ride into Lane City an' find you a preacha', sho'nuf. You white folks can honeymoon in style, and I's goin' to have a lot mo' room in my lil' cabin heah." He ducked out the door then back in again. "Do you mind if I borrow one of these fine steeds you brought back, Danny Boy?"

"Take whichever one you want and scoot."

Rebecca looked even more confused. "André seems different than I expected. He doesn't seem at all afraid of you."

"Afraid? André? Why in the Sam Hill should he be afraid of me? When we were kids he could whoop my … posterior. Might still be able to." Daniel shrugged.

"You were his *owner*. He was a piece of property to you?"

"Whoa, lady. I think you have a bit of a New England perception of the way things run in the South. Most of us were raised by our mammy. Since we weren't very rich when I came along, André's mother acted as my mammy. If I misbehaved, she would whip me, not the other way around. When I fell and skinned my knee, she was right there to bandage it." Dan continued, "You've read too much of Mrs. Stowe's *Uncle Tom's Cabin*. Most of us in the South consider the Negros on our plantations as our people. I've come to look at the evil side of slavery differently since I left Louisiana. That's why I freed André. Still, he will always be one of 'my people.'"

She shrugged. "He's strange. He can speak perfect English when he wants. I don't understand him. Sometimes he defers to you, then other times he acts, well, bossy."

Daniel laughed. "I think you New Englanders are the ones who want to keep Negros 'in their place.' We Southerners know if we are friends with a Negro and he with us, it is a stronger bond than slavery – for both of us. A plantation slave knows when he is too old to work, he will have a roof over his head, plenty of food and nursing by the owner's wife when he is sick. Can your factory workers back east say the same?"

"Mr. Fitzgerald, those people make their place in this world. The Lord designed it so."

"Why, Miss Becky, I declare, I've heard plantation owners say the same thing. Come on, grab one of those stale biscuits and an apple. Let's go look over your new domain."

After a hasty wash up with a bucket of water André must have brought up from the nearby creek, they headed over to inspect the Doyles' vacated cabin. They walked the distance between the two cabins, a little less than a mile, in thoughtful silence.

Rebecca was trying to understand the strange, to her at least, relationship between this man she had pledged to marry and his unusual former slave. She had had some slight dealings with Negros who were domestics or workers who were expected to defer to people like her and her father who were educated and reasonably well-to-do. She knew, too, there was a strong political movement to ban freedmen from homesteading in Kansas as Dan had correctly noted about the Topeka Constitution. She sincerely hoped reasonable men like Governor Robinson would be able to change that.

Now she was seeing a certain hypocrisy in her thoughts and behavior with regard to Negros. She considered herself a liberal person and certainly superior to Southern planters who held these people in captivity and considered them less than human, yet she could not deny some truth in Daniel's words. Many Northerners, especially lower class workers, did not like colored people and only objected to slavery because it limited jobs for them.

André was a puzzle to her. Thankfully, it was one she did not have to solve at the moment. The enigma she must deal with at once was Daniel. She was going to marry this man. She wasn't naive enough to believe they could share a cabin for any length of time without intimacy. She admitted to herself she felt a certain tingle when he touched her. Her thoughts buzzed through her head like hornets in a nest.

When she had arrived in Lawrence with her father, she had believed that place primitive. This was something she had never envisioned.

How could humans live under these conditions? How would she manage? Her home in Lawrence was clapboard frame and had separate bedrooms. The kitchen was separated from the main house by a dogtrot, and there was an adequate privy out back. Even after her father's death when Nathan and Laura had taken her in, she shared a room with her best friend, Lydia. She had all the modern conveniences.

Now through one stupid and impulsive act, she had condemned herself to a life in this archaic backwater. It was not a stupid act, she chided herself. It was necessary for her to do as she did it to appease her conscience. How could she have lived with herself if this enchanting man had been hanged because of her?

Dan cast a sidelong glance at this appealing woman by his side. How had he gotten into this predicament? True, she was a beautiful lady and he did feel very attracted to her; however, he had known many other beautiful women he had been attracted to in the past. The only time the word "marriage" had been bandied about was last year when he had become a little too intimate with Desiree Thibodaux.

Desiree had been a few months older than him and quite beautiful with her flashing black eyes and mane of black curls that tumbled over a white pillow like a man's dream of heaven. She had been more than willing to engage in a little bit of late night fun. Then, after a few clandestine meetings, she broached the subject of marriage. "Danny, we are so o o good together, are we not? Perhaps we should marry so we could be together always and not have to sneak around to meet."

For the then-seventeen-year-old Dan, sneaking around was part of the fun. The word "marry" had the effect of a pin against his balloon of excitement. He did what he had done since childhood: went to his father. Michael told him to take a few days to go visit New Orleans. When he returned, Desiree announced her engagement to another local lad. Although Dan's pride was stung to realize she might have been cavorting with others at the same time, his overwhelming feeling was relief. He believed he was too young. Now here he was again, this time actively planning to marry a stranger.

He broke the silence with a comment he was not sure was directed at Becky or himself. "You know I do have to leave for however long it takes to catch Old Brown and his murdering band?"

Only Becky's eyes hinted at how painful the thought was of Dan fighting against an abolitionist. "I understand."

Daniel and Becky stepped into the clearing in front of the cabin. It was simple but much more impressive than the hurried structure Daniel and André shared. Rebecca's spirits lifted when they entered the dwelling. It was small by Lawrence standards, about twelve by twenty-four feet and was divided into two rooms.

The single door opened into a combination dining and indoor kitchen with a window on both the front and rear walls. The massive fireplace built of stone and clay dominated the wall to their left. A large Dutch oven and kettle hung over the hearth, and a few utensils sat on the large hand-crafted table. The floor was wide hewn planks.

The timber-framed ceiling was peaked with a loft covering the area over the second room, a bedroom. A sturdy ladder led to the loft, probably where the Doyle children had slept. In the bedroom, a massive rope bed occupied one corner. The mattress seemed to be well-stuffed. A few blankets still remained on it. A bench stood under the room's only window. A few clothing pegs hung on the wall. Something, probably a storage chest, had been moved from the other side. In the Doyles' haste, some garments had been abandoned.

Rebecca picked up one dingy dress from the middle of the floor. "At least I'll have a change of clothing until I can get settled in." She held the dress in front of her. It would have covered her twice, but nonetheless she was happy to find such a treasure. She checked the seams and calculated how to alter it to fit. As she looked around the bare room, she was filled with joy. She had no complaints. She was about to marry a man she found attractive and would have a home of her own. All her other worries fell away. "I can make us a real home here, Mr. Fitzgerald."

Daniel smiled. "If we are going to wed, you need to call me Dan, Danny or anything. Mr. Fitzgerald, that's my father."

She smiled up at him. "Oh yes, Dan, we will make this strange union of ours something wonderful."

Danny reached out and stroked her curls. "Yes, we will." He leaned close to plant a kiss on her lips, which was interrupted by a series of sharp yips outside the door. They both rushed outside to find a pair of brown and white hound pups. The dogs were as surprised to see them as they were to see the dogs. The confused pups backed up and tumbled over themselves in their haste to escape the intruders.

Danny tried to catch the larger of the pair, but the little dog ducked under his arm. Becky made a grab at the closest hind leg. The surprised pup stopped struggled and began licking the hand that held him prisoner. The smaller one gave up without a struggle. Eventually, Danny and Becky managed to trap the little fellows in the small pen behind the outhouse.

A little petting and a stale biscuit made friends of the two pups. They were at that awkward stage, all legs and paws. Only the liquid brown eyes gazing trustingly at the new humans betrayed their fear. Those humans, of course, were instantly won over. Daniel repeated what Mrs. Doyle had told him about the mother dog being stabbed to death in Brown's attack and her belief that the pups had also been killed. "They must have been frightened off before the raiders could kill them."

"Oh, Dan, let's name them Mason and Dixon in honor of our origins." Not keeping them wasn't even considered.

By the time they had returned to Daniel's cabin, André rode up with a middle-aged clergyman. "I found you a preacher and also a message from Captain Pate. He needs you to ride into Ottawa City tonight with the reverend, here. They are forming up there to make an attack on Osawatomie and arrest John Brown."

After introductions, the preacher, Reverend Martin White, performed a hasty ceremony. In spite of Becky's soiled black dress, Danny thought her the prettiest bride he had ever seen. Postponing the honeymoon was going to test his will power.

Immediately after the ceremony, the groom gathered his newly acquired rifle, which he had named Little Thunder, and some meager provisions and rode his new palomino off into the night with Martin White, leaving his bride and their two newly acquired puppies under the care of André. His thoughts strayed back to an image of Becky, her hair loose and clad in a flimsy shift lying alone in bed on their wedding night. He sent a loving thought winging back through the night. *I will make things better for you, I swear.*

 Chapter Four

May 29, 1856—Franklin County, Kansas Territory

When Dan and Reverend Martin White arrived in camp they found it in a state of confusion. Although it was after midnight, men milled around. It looked more like a gathering of outlaws instead of a territorial militia unit. Several large tents seemed to form sleeping accommodations for groups of men. Here and there individual regulation tents were set in no discernable pattern.

Dan had to ask several times to be directed to Captain Pate's tent. He finally spotted James Harris talking to some other militiamen.

"Good seeing you here, Mr. Harris." Daniel guided the two horses toward his neighbor. "I was afraid you had pulled up stakes after your close call."

"Hello, Daniel, Reverend White. I *will* be taking my family back to Missouri after we catch Old Brown," Harris replied. "Sad business. I feel for the wives and children. Mrs. Doyle left yet?"

"Yes, she did," Dan replied. "We're here to help catch Brown too. Where do we report?"

Harris directed them to a harried officer trying to cope with the bedlam around him. Since neither Martin nor Dan, along with many of the other recruits, had their own tents, Pate's young lieutenant, John Brockett, assigned Dan and Martin to his own tent and instructed them, "We ride out first thing tomorrow. Be ready at dawn."

In the tent they met a few other militiamen. The feeling was one of celebration. All assembled seemed to believe they would easily capture Brown, his sons and the rest of the murderers. A stone jug was making its rounds, adding to the conviviality of the group.

One of the men reported the rumor Brown had acted under direct orders from James Lane. That spurred several stories of Lane's antics. Dan learned that Lane often led a band of freebooters and raiders. He had fought in the Mexican War and understood tactics, making him a dangerous adversary.

Feeling accepted by this diverse group, Dan recounted his narrow escape from Lane in Lawrence.

"Ya made a bad enemy, friend. That man is meaner than a cornered rattlesnake with a toothache, and he can talk his way out of hell," a young trooper named James Turner stated.

"He don't need to talk his way out of Hell. Him and the Devil are best friends," a lieutenant named Iverson countered.

Finally, the men settled in for the night. They knew first light would arrive soon and they would be on the road toward Paola.

⬸

Becky awoke with a start and gazed around at the unfamiliar surroundings. It took her a minute to realize she was in Mrs. Doyle's old bed in this little cabin far removed from anyone and everything familiar. Even her name was new and strange. *Mrs. Rebecca Fitzgerald.* She considered herself lucky in spite of it all. Her father had often warned her to think before acting, but she knew no matter how long she had considered her actions in regard to freeing Dan, she would have done the same thing. She considered herself a good judge of people, and Lane had always felt intrinsically evil to her. Lane's parting threat caused a cold chill to race over her body in spite of the warm spring weather. He would not forget what she had done, and he was a powerful man in Kansas. Dan from the beginning had come across as a good person even though they had different beliefs. At least they agreed on the slavery issue. *Enough lying abed like a sluggard*, she told herself.

Her next surprise awaited her in the front room. André had apparently been up early and brought over a supply of food and drawn a bucket of water from the well in the front yard. The gesture, though appreciated, raised another question in Becky's already overactive mind. Did he think he needed to serve her?

She was disabused of that awkward thought when André tapped at the door with a line of freshly caught fish in hand. "I caught a mess of fish this morning, so it's only fair you cook us breakfast," he informed her.

Becky almost replied, "Yes, sir." She didn't want him to feel he was her servant, but it appeared that was not something he considered. At the same time, she was not sure how she should address him. An educated Negro who was not in any way intimidated made her a little nervous. She settled for a simple, "Thank you. I will be glad to cook the fish." She took the string. "What should I call you?"

André busied himself starting a fire in the stone fireplace. "Well, Rebecca, André has been my name as long as I remember, so I guess that is what you can call me."

Becky blushed. The matter seemed settled. She cleaned the fish, saving the heads and entrails for Mason and Dixon, and proceeded to use some of the flour and spices on the table to coat the rest. She scoped out a few spoonfuls of lard to put in the Dutch oven André had placed on its hook and swung over the flame. "A spider for frying would be nice, but this Dutch oven will do. I guess Mrs. Doyle didn't have room for too much. She must have been very frightened to leave all these things."

André looked up from the blazing fire. "If you had seen her husband and boys, you would have been frightened, too."

For the first time, it occurred to Becky *she* might have something to fear from the very people she once felt were her friends. She had met Old John Brown and two of his sons once at a meeting in Lawrence. Brown senior, tall and gaunt with a square jaw and blazing eyes, had seemed fierce, almost biblical to her. Young John Junior had seemed somewhat unbalanced and strange. The other son, Fredrick, in spite of his large size, had seemed the kindest of the trio although a bit slow-witted.

While Becky cooked the fish over the fireplace and made a kettle of coffee with the beans André had brought over. André set two places at the table. She told him about finding the two pups.

"I saw them outside but thought maybe you brought them with you from Lawrence."

As they ate, he informed her he was going into town and pick up some supplies. He added the spider she needed to the list and asked if she needed anything else. "I can't take you as we now have only one dray horse, Trouble, and one riding horse here. The wagon is set up to be pulled by two and I don't think these two will do well hitched together until they get better acquainted."

Embarrassed because she had no money, Becky mumbled "No."

André gave her an exasperated look. "Look, I know you people from up north have some funny ideas about what is proper. Ever since you first met me, you have been tippy-toeing around as if I might scalp you. Forget the fact my skin is a little darker than yours. Forget all of that hogwash you learned up north about us 'poor abused darkies,' and try and see me simply as another human being and your husband's br... best friend."

It was the 'you people' that set Becky's back up. "People up north are not devils as you seem to think. We want Negros to be free and get an education."

"Well, I'm free and I have an excellent education, and you seem to have a problem with me."

"I am so sorry," Becky replied. "In actual practice I'm not used to being around free educated Negros. You're a good friend to Dan and I'm married to him, and I have so much to learn about this new life. I think you could help me a lot if you wanted, and I do want us to be friends, André."

"Good that's more like it." Strong white teeth flashed against his pale-tan skin. "And for the record, slaves should be freed. I think many people in the South know it, and it will happen. It can't happen soon enough to suit me. I hope it happens without bloodshed, but I doubt it will. Too much money at stake, and people are awfully touchy about letting go of money or money producers. You people are not too far off the mark about schooling. Education will be vital. Right now the field hands would be in terrible straits if they were suddenly cast adrift in that frail craft called freedom. Still they would at least be free to make their own destiny. Blacksmiths, cooks, builders and those slaves with a skill would have an advantage. Many of us need to learn that freedom has a big price tag. Right now, most slaves expect 'Massa' to take care of us in hard times. With our freedom would come the need to be able to take care of ourselves. Still, even with all the problems, freedom is every colored person's dream."

"Well said, André. However if we are going to be friends, you need to stop saying 'you people' I don't consider myself at all one with people like Jim Lane or John Brown."

"Amen to that. I agree with you there. Those two are bad medicine." He grinned, "Now, I'll ask you again. What do you need in town?"

Becky smiled back at her friend. "Actually, I do need a few things. I have to make some dresses, and I'll need lots of kitchen equipment and other things. I'll make you a list."

After André left, she went out to feed and get more acquainted with Mason and Dixon. Food was the magic button. They seemed to accept her totally. She petted them and stroked their silky long ears. They rolled and tumbled and chased one another around the dirt front yard. *Now if only the neighbors will do the same,* she thought. *Why do people have to let regional differences decide who are friends and who must be an enemy?*

 Chapter Five

May 29, 1856—Franklin County, Kansas Territory

Sunrise presaged one of those warm, sunny spring days Kansas could offer in reparation for the dreary storm a scant few days ago. John Brockett assigned Dan to ride with a detail led by Martin White. Orders were to check out any known abolitionists' strongholds and search for John Brown or any of his men.

"Mount up, men," Martin shouted, "we're heading north toward Paola. Let's see if we can flush out Brown and his men."

They rode in single file along a poorly defined trail across prairie terrain filled with early blooming sunflowers, yucca plants and dozens of wildflowers Dan had never seen before mingled with tall prairie grasses painting a landscape alive with golden color accented by red, green and brown. The smell of sagebrush drifted on every passing breeze.

Much as Dan enjoyed the scenery, he chaffed at the delays caused by stopping at every tiny hamlet to question people about strangers passing through several nights ago. Most of the man they met were from Missouri and pro-South. Any of the Free-State settlements were poorer by a few saddlebags full of loot after the scouting party left. Most of the locals invited the militiamen to share meals, and several times they were offered a few swigs from jugs that contained a particularly virulent form of local corn whiskey called White Mule. The name fit, Dan thought; the raw hooch had a kick like a contrary mule. A few of the men even joined up to help catch Brown.

That night they made camp near Paola. After a day of meeting friendly villagers and sharing food and whisky, the men were sloppy about sentry duty and many slept in the open without even setting up the tents. Pate seemed to be unconcerned with maintaining a semblance of discipline. Dan, Martin and several of the men pitched their large shared tent.

The next morning, the early risers, mostly the men who had not imbibed too freely the day before, fixed a hasty breakfast. Martin had orders to take a small squad of men and search the area around Osawatomie. As they rode away from camp, Martin called to Dan, "Ride up front with me, boy. I noticed on the way here you pick up trail signs pretty well. You seem to have a good sense of direction in the woods too. Might make a first-class scout out of you."

Dan grinned. "When you grow up in Louisiana with swamps, lakes and the Mississippi River around, you either get a good sense of direction or you don't survive."

Martin grunted his approval, and they rode awhile mostly in silence. Martin pointed out some local facts. Dan already knew the cottonwood trees grew along creeks or riverbeds, so their shimmering triangular leaves were a good indicator water was near. An important thing to know in a dry prairie area like Kansas. He also learned come fall the leaves would take on a bright yellow color visible for miles because of the stark contrast with the blue of the Kansas sky. Dan had not realized the tree had males and females; only the females produced the small, white cotton-like pods that brought forth a new tree. "Don't let one take root near any of your fields," Martin cautioned. "They have a big, nasty root system, and it spreads over almost an acre. Gets brittle and splits in storms, too."

Martin changed the subject. "None of my business, but I can't help noticing your bride has a decided New England accent. Folks like us get a little suspicious of Yankees. The way things are in the territory, a man's got to know he can trust his friends and their family."

"I know I can trust Rebecca with my life." Dan gave Martin an abbreviated version of the events in Lawrence.

"Well, I guess that does make her trustworthy," Martin acknowledged. "Just don't like that accent."

"Why do people have to be judged by where they come from? Or even by the color of their skin?"

Martin gave him a stern look. "You go talking like that, folks 'round here are going to think you're a damned abolitionist. In Kansas Territory, and I suspect all over the country before long, a man's got to take a stand on one side or the other of this slavery issue. The Kansas-Nebraska Act makes it impossible for anyone not to take sides."

Dan nodded. "I heard about it but never really understood the significance until lately. In Louisiana, it didn't have much impact."

"Well, in Missouri it sure as hell has a lot of impact. Congress and everyone else naturally figured Kansas would be a slave state and Nebraska a free one. It made sense because of location and a sense of fairness. White shook his head. "Missouri can't afford to have any more free states close by where negras can run away to. It's bad enough the Indian Territory, Illinois and Iowa are next door to it, but Missouri is not going to sit still and let Kansas go Free-State too. As long as everybody knew the way it was, Kansas slave and Nebraska free, everybody was happy."

"Yeah, I understand, but it is sure creating a ruckus."

White shrugged. "When them damned fools in Washington decided they didn't want to dirty their hands with a decision to make Kansas a slave state, Douglas figured it was an easy way to not have to take responsibility. Let the territories vote. Results would be the same since Missouri people would naturally move into Kansas Territory and keep the balance we need, and Congress could play Pilate and 'Let someone else decide.'"

"So now we have to fight it out here with New Englanders who want to throw off that balance. I don't like slavery, but for now, cotton states need the cheap labor. Pity there isn't some way to end it so both races get a fair deal. We have to deal with it eventually. Let the North deal with the labor laws and the terrible conditions the Irish immigrants live under up there," Dan continued.

"I was always taught the Bible itself sanctions slavery. Don't know much about labor conditions up North. I always reckoned that was the Yankees' business," White admitted.

Dan smiled wryly. "It's almost as bad as slavery. Emigrants, especially Irish ones, can't make a living and can only hold the most menial jobs. Why, in Boston, many businesses needing workers have signs posted 'Irish need not apply.' That's the same *Boston* that sent many of its citizens down here to tell *us* how inhumane *we are* to our slaves. I heard they refused to even let a ship from Cork, Ireland, the *Mary*, land and disembark its forty-six Irish passengers a few years back."

"Goes to show it doesn't take color of skin to cause people to be treated unfairly. I don't own any slaves myself. Pro-Slave is a handy catchword for those of us who are 'sound on the goose.' Slavery is not what I'm fighting for, but it's part and parcel of our Southern way of life. I will not let anyone tell my state what we can or can't do." Martin set his jaw and looked straight ahead, closing the subject.

As they neared the small settlement, they spotted a man trudging down the road. He walked with his head down and seemed to be shivering as if he had a fever. As they neared the traveler, he hailed them and inquired, "Is this the way to Ottawa Jones' place?

Martin White pulled his pistol and pointed it at the stranger. "We hit pay dirt here," he shouted back to the rest of the troop. "None other than Jason Brown." Addressing the traveler, he demanded, "You're one of Old Brown's sons, aren't you? You were one of the bunch who killed the Doyles, Mr. Sherman and Mr. Wilkerson."

The stranger studied Martin for a few beats. "I believe I remember you from a cattle stealing party that raided around Osawatomie and pressed a bunch of our cows and horses a while ago."

Dan noted Martin did not contradict Brown. "I asked who you are, boy," Martin barked.

Brown squared his shoulders. "Yes, I am John Brown's son, Jason. I am what you Missourians call an abolitionist. If you want to kill me for what I believe, go ahead. I never murdered your friends. I am a peaceful farmer in Osawatomie and never knowingly hurt any human being. I have not seen my father in several days."

"Rest easy, Brown. We are not like your father and his band. We will bring you back to camp and turn you over to our commander."

On Martin's orders, two of the militiamen dismounted and tied a lead rope to the prisoner's hands to pull him along.

Martin led his men with their prisoners to a place near the town of Paola where Captain Pate had led a party of men to search for any of Brown's men and any stray valuables or horses belonging to the Free-Staters they might stumble upon. Pate was thrilled with the prize of Jason Brown. Some of the men were for hanging Brown on the spot, but reason prevailed. The discussion so upset Brown that he began running a fever. Judge Jacobs, Judge Cato and some others who had met with Pate to see if any progress was being made agreed it was best to hold Jason Brown at Judge Jacobs' home until a trial could be set.

Ironically, Mrs. Doyle and her children were also guests at the judge's home. Dinner that night was a strained affair. The judge and his family, Mrs. Doyle, about forty pro-slavery men including militia and civilians and Jason Brown broke bread together. Dan did get chance to tell Mrs. Doyle of his marriage and of finding the two pups. She was happy to hear the pups had not been killed but a little less enthusiastic about Dan's new bride.

The next morning, a group of scouts who had been scouring the other side of the area returned to camp with another prize. They had found John Brown, Jr. His captors were chuckling over John Junior's antics. Even as the men led the prisoner into camp, he shouted, "Look sharp, men. I am commanding you to stop this foolishness. I said listen to me. I am your commander and need to be respected."

Junior continued his senseless babble even as he was led into Pate's presence. The man seemed to think he was in his own camp and in command of the troops.

Since he was acting erratically, Pate ordered him confined with an old ox chain they had discovered near the judge's cabin. Jason's fever had worsened overnight, so he was confined in one of the judge's bedrooms.

Later in the day, Captain Woods of the U.S. Army Dragoons approached the camp. Captain Woods was a stickler for order and demanded strict military discipline. He rode over and saluted Pate. "Captain, since I am regular military and you are militia, I will herewith take command of those prisoners."

Pate had no option but to accept the decision. "Certainly, Sir."

He ordered several militiamen to bring the prisoners forth and turn them over to Woods. In an effort to appear professional, Pate attempted to exact more proper demeanor among his small troop. The drinking and looting temporarily stopped.

The army and militia troops marched together until they approached Middle Ottawa Creek early on Saturday morning. Here Captain Woods decided to set up camp before continuing on toward Lecompton.

Captain Pate rode on a ways farther, decided to set up camp at Black Jack Campground, a place used by travelers heading west on the Santa Fe Trail between Palmyra and Prairie City. Both of these towns were Free-State strongholds.

Pate called out, "We'll set up camp here and do a bit of reconnaissance for a few days to see if we can flush murdering Old Brown out."

Pate showed the first bit of military knowledge Dan had seen since the operation began. A little stream called Captain's Creek forked out into an inverted "Y" here. He ordered them to bivouac directly in front of a wooded ravine filled with shallow water from the eastern branch of the creek and had them set up the wagons in a line in front of their position to form a makeshift breastwork. There was a nice grassy area to the south of their position, almost midway between the two tiny streams, where they could tether the horses.

Dan found a good spot with plenty of grass and a tiny rivulet. It was a little closer to their camp than most of the other animals were positioned. Dan tethered Chieftain, as he had named the palomino, and gave him a quick rub down. "The Grim Chieftain" was one of Lane's nicknames, so Dan felt it was an appropriate name.

After everyone had set up the tents, Pate ordered Martin to do some reconnaissance. Martin called out to whoever wished to ride with him, "Boys, let's go check out Palmyra. We know it's a hell-hole of Free-Staters."

Again Dan rode ahead with the preacher. Martin was companionable but silent. After a restless night, Dan had come to terms with the facts of war. He knew he was inexperienced and put aside his misgivings about the looting. As he told himself, *It's being done to us Southerners by people like Lane and Brown. We need to retaliate.*

Pretty soon they arrived at a clearing, and the rest of the troop came up behind and stopped to look things over. There were five cabins and a small general store a ways down the road but still in sight. A man plowing a field with a team of mules saw the strangers and turned to await them. He held a large machete in his right hand and an old shotgun leaned against the fence.

"How do, sir," Martin greeted the man. "We're part of the Westport Sharpshooters Militia and hunting some criminals. Have you seen any strangers around lately?"

The farmer looked over the small group. He spat in front of Dan's horse's hooves. "Ayah? Looks to me like *youh* strangers around heah. Yah ain't gettin' no help from us trackin' God-feahin' folk like John Brown. Bettah get youhselves outah heah and go back South wheah yah can buy and sell people like cattle." The man dropped his machete and reached for his shotgun but never completed the move. One of the militiamen behind Dan fired a shot that sent the man sprawling. Before any help could arrive, the troop began firing randomly at the other figures emerging from the nearby cabins. The rest of the locals, seeing they were outgunned if not outnumbered, raised their hands and made no move to defend themselves.

The whole incident happened fast and caught Dan by surprise. The dead settler obviously was a free-state man. His accent and belligerence gave him away at once, but Dan felt the militiamen reacted too harshly. He had no time to reason it through. Martin threw him a length of rope and yelled, "Dan, tie up those prisoners. James," Martin indicated one of the other riders, "help Dan cover the abolitionists so nobody gets brave and tries to commit suicide. The rest of you men help me check out the general store. Mighty funny no one there stuck their noses out."

Dan tied the seven men standing in the street then returned to his horse to take his place guarding the prisoners. James went to search the cabins for any stragglers who had not come out. The bound men said little and made no escape attempt. Just as well, as Dan did not know if he could have fired on any of them if they had. When James returned, Dan noticed he carried a bag bulging with tools and knives. Seeing Dan's stare, James laughed. "My hardship pay for rounding up these scum. You want to see if they have anything you need in there?"

Dan shook his head. He still felt that the looting was wrong. It bothered him.

In a short time, Martin White and the rest of the troop returned from the store. They led two men who had their arms tied behind them. One seemed resigned to his fate, but the other was yelling, "Let me go! I tell ya I'm yust an honest shopkeeper. Yust minding mine own business."

Martin informed the troops, "The quiet fellow was riding down

35

the road toward the store and has letters from a journalist who was with Old Brown recently. He claims to be a Baptist preacher, name of Moore. The other fellow is a German named Winer." He cast a sour look at the vocal prisoner. "Sure lives up to his name. He's generally obnoxious, but he may have been on the raid with Old Brown. Says Brown is nearby and about to capture us. We found a keg of gunpowder in the store. Take it down the road a bit and set it off so the damned abolitionists can't use it against us. Also set the store on fire."

The little troop headed back to camp with their prisoners to report their findings. Dan noticed most of the men had filled knapsacks with plunder. Even the reverend had somewhat bulging pockets.

"What about these men, Rev?" James Turner asked, indicating the bound men they had captured first.

"Leave them be," White replied. "Some of their less adventurous friends will pop out of the woods and release them after we leave. These two seem to have some knowledge of where Brown may be hiding out. May even be relatives of Brown–he has eighteen sons, so half the county may be related to him–according to the only person in the store who was willing to speak to us other than cursing us for Missouri Ruffians."

Dan hung back near the rear on the ride back. Martin dropped back to talk with him. "I know this seems a bit harsh to you, Dan, but it's the way war is done. And make no mistake, this is war. Those men would have put a bullet through any Southerner sure as a rattlesnake strikes. Remember, these rascals are in cahoots with John Brown. They agree with what he did to your friends the Doyles and the other victims. Anything we take from them is not stealing. It is keeping money and supplies out of the hands of men like John Brown."

"Put like that, I guess I do understand," Dan allowed, keeping his doubts to himself.

As they rode off, he started when he heard an explosion. Just the gunpowder keg, he realized.

When they arrived back at camp, Lieutenant Brockett informed them they had to wait to deliver their prisoners to the captain. "Captain Pate is interrogating one of the prisoners another group brought in a little while ago, a doctor from Prairie City named Graham. He's saying Brown and a Free State militia captain named Shore have teamed up to hunt for us."

Martin gestured at his prisoners. "What do you want me to do with these fellows? They may have some information too. Old Moore has letters from a reporter about Brown's whereabouts. I didn't want to take it on myself to open them, but I think Captain Pate will be interested in them."

"Coleman's groups flushed out a few prisoners worth holding along with this Doctor Graham, and we've set up a tent with some guards over yonder." Brockett pointed to an exposed spot with a single large tent. "Put your prisoners there, and as soon as the captain is free, I'll call you to report. Chances are he is going to be very interested in your prisoners as well."

No sooner had Dan and Martin secured their prisoners in the tent than Pate called them over. White saluted half-heartedly and handed Pate the two letters. Pate was so enraged by one which called him so many unflattering names that he threw it in the fire without finishing it. The other, obviously intended for publication and called "Confessions of a Horse Thief," was so ludicrous that Pate ordered Lieutenant Coleman to read it to the troops. It was a windy document praising Brown and denouncing Pate and all Southerners. The language was so insulting, some of the men suggested hanging the journalist as well as Brown when he was captured.

All the men went to bed that night laughing and in very high spirits. They awoke the next morning in a very different mood.

 Chapter 6

June 2, 1856—Blackjack Campground, Kansas Territory

As the sun was breaking over the horizon and shafting through the open tent flap, a single shot cracked through Dan's dream. He jolted awake. For a second he wanted to recapture the pleasant dream that included Becky and a well-stuffed mattress. He rubbed his eyes and quickly grasped the situation. His mattress was not at all comfortable, just a folded blanket on hard ground. His nearest companion was not Becky but Martin White. All around him men were grabbing their guns. Something was happening outside. Dan grasped his Sharp's rifle and ran for the tent flap.

The dawn light revealed a fearsome sight. Directly across from their encampment men were taking position and firing. Dan had a quick glimpse of John Brown and another man apparently arguing. The second man seemed to be the commander of a portion of the Free-State militiamen, probably Captain Shore. As Dan watched horrified, Brown seemed to be sending Shore toward the point of the Y where Shore's men could fire down the ravine directly into their ranks.

"They're going to have us in their crossfire," Dan whispered to Martin as they took their position at the end of the improvised breastworks behind the last wagon near the south end.

"We're dead if they do," Martin replied while both men fired and reloaded as fast as they could. Some of the other militiamen seemed to grasp the situation and were also sending a steady volley into the enemy line.

"Look! Shore is going to rush us head on instead." Dan couldn't believe this piece of stupidity. Even as inexperienced as he was, he realized what would happen to Shore's men.

Within seconds, about a dozen men followed Captain Shore in a direct charge across the open prairie in front of them. Martin and Dan grinned at one another and both took aim at the advancing enemy. Two of the advancing troopers fell under the Southerners' steady fire. Their comrades helped the wounded men to their feet, and all of them fell back to take shelter in a wooded area behind them. This put them out of range, but the fierce attack had wreaked havoc on the Southern line in an unexpected way. Dan watched as almost half of the Southern men dashed for their horses and mules.

"Cowards!" Martin shouted, shaking his left fist as he stopped to reload.

"Don't be too hard on them. Most of them have never been under fire before. Street fights and saloon brawls aren't the same thing." Dan admonished. His insides were quaking as the bullets passed over his head. "I admit I'm scared, too."

"A man's got to be crazy not to be frightened when he's being shot at. But if you're a man, you stand your ground and don't desert your friends."

The tempo of firing from the other side picked up speed. With a sinking heart, Dan realized Brown and some of his men were now gunning down the Southerners' mounts. Frightened squeals and brays of agony arose as the horses and mules fell under the steady fusillade. Dan was thankful Chieftain was far to the back and hopefully out of range of Brown's men.

Martin grimaced. "Brown is not letting any more of our men run away. He is feeling pretty sure of the outcome here."

Dan looked over his shoulder toward the rest of the troop. He nudged Martin. "Pate just signaled us to pull back to the ravine behind the camp."

As they joined the other men retreating to safer ground, Dan could see three men who appeared wounded. He was close enough to one of them to smell the odor of blood and hear the man moan. Dan's quivering stomach was beginning to feel steadier. In fact he felt a certain pride in having stood fast with his friends and not running away like a frightened rabbit. *Fitzgerald, with a little luck you might live to walk away from your first battle. You have seen the elephant.*

Dan knelt with the butt of his rifle, Little Thunder, pressed to his shoulder. The gun spoke with a deep roar. The rhythm had become automatic by now. Fire. Reload. Fire. Reload. Smoke blanketed the field, and the smell of burned power stung his nostrils. Up and down the line, all the militiamen were concentrating on the battle. It was becoming easier not to think that one of his bullets could kill a fellow human being. Then Dan remembered Drury Doyle, and he no longer cared if he killed one of *these* men.

Actually, not many bullets were finding targets on either side. Dan heard very few rumbling sounds such as his Sharp's rifle made. He knew only two of the Southern militiamen besides him had these long-range guns and guessed that the Free-State side had about the same number.

No one was prepared for what happened next. Later Dan would

wonder at the rider's courage or stupidly, but for the moment he was stunned into inaction as a large solitary horseman rode across his field of vision.

The rider came out of nowhere and galloped directly between the firing troops. "Father, we have them surrounded! Help has arrived."

He heard someone down the line mutter, "That's Fredrick Brown. He is a bit simple-minded."

Another man commented, "A bit? I would say downright daft to do that."

Suddenly the firing stilled. Pate signaled that he wanted to parley. Dan knew his ammunition was getting low and suspected the other men were in the same situation. Pate sent over Lieutenant Brockett and one of the prisoners under a flag of truce. Dan could see them make their way carefully across the open prairie to Brown's position, their white flag held high. Dan watched Brown continue shaking his head, and eventually the two men returned.

The twenty-three uninjured men remaining in the Southern troop clustered around Pate waiting to see what Brown wanted.

"Captain, Old Brown says he won't parley with no 'un but you," Brockett stated.

"Well, I reckon I'll go see what the crazy coot wants. I figure if we stall long enough, we might get some reinforcements. It should be easy to get him talking. He loves to hear his own voice." Pate handed his rifle to Brockett and proceeded toward enemy lines.

Within minutes, Dan was horrified as he watched Brown place a gun to Pate's head and demanded everyone shut up and surrender. It was a violation of a flag of truce. Besides, Brown was assaulting a federal officer as Pate had been sworn in as a U.S. Marshal and issued a warrant to arrest Brown before they began their quest. Still, that gun in Brown's hand overruled all other considerations. It was surrender or see their captain shot in cold blood. Dan scanned the tense faces of his fellow warriors. It was clear not a man among them doubted Brown would not hesitate to pull that trigger.

Slowly each of them laid their rifles at their feet.

"Your pistols too," Brown commanded, "and don't forget them Missouri Toothpicks you Southerons are so fond of."

A low rumble of dissent passed through the Southern lines, but the troopers complied with Brown's order. Dan reluctantly laid down his Little Thunder. When the pile of guns and Bowie knives filled the ground at the Southerners' feet, Brown ordered them to back away. "Go tie their hands behind them," he commanded several of his men. "We're going to offer them some Osawatomie hospitality." He cast a contemptuous glance at his fellow commander. "Shore, take a few boys and release our men these slavers captured," Brown directed the other militia captain. Although equal in rank, Shore obeyed without a question.

"Brown," Pate said, "I've got three wounded soldiers. It would be inhumane to take them prisoner and march them all over the prairie."

Brown's eyes burned over his prisoner. "*Captain* Pate, if reporters like you are going to play at soldiering, you need to at least get the ranks and protocol correct. You address an officer by his rank," Brown almost smiled, "especially when you are that officer's prisoner and he is holding a gun on you."

Pate's helpless fury was clear in his expression, but his voice was even."*Captain* Brown, what about my wounded men?"

"Of course." Brown called out to one of his men, "Send the wounded slavers to Prairie City with Dr. Graham. He can tend their wounds." Brown turned back to Pate. "Never let it be said that John Brown was inhumane."

Dan couldn't control the words that leapt from his mouth. "I suppose what you did to the Doyles and the others wasn't *inhumane*?"

Brown turned to face Dan. "Come here, boy."

Dan considered refusing just on principle but decided that would be foolish as Brown's men surrounded them brandishing loaded rifles while he was unarmed.

Dan stepped forward and stood facing the old man. "You slaughtered five unarmed men. I call that inhumane. What do you call it?"

"That was a direct command from a higher authority," Brown replied.

"Would that *higher authority* be James Lane?"

The eyes staring back at Dan were brown, deep set and riveting. Looking into those dark orbs, Dan was sure he faced a complete madman. Brown's answer confirmed his worst fears. "I spoke directly to God, and He ordered the sacrifice of those slavers. Colonel Lane naturally concurred that it was necessary."

Dusk was falling when Brown called a halt. "Untie the prisoners' hands so they can set up their tents."

Apparently Brown's men had no tents. The captives were herded to a slightly wooded area and allowed to relieve themselves while under the watchful guns of the abolitionists. There were a few snickers and ungentlemanly comments related to anatomy and size, but for the most part the Southerners were allowed to take care of business in peace.

Next Brown's men directed the prisoners to set up the tents in the middle of the clearing. Brown led them in a long-winded prayer. Only then were they allowed to eat. Dan sat next to Captain Pate around a small campfire. When Dan had met Pate, he admired the captain who was only a few years older than himself. Now his only feeling was pity.

"Hard to believe an old man like Brown could trick us like that," Dan said in a low voice.

"Yes, but I should never have gone into his camp myself. I should have known that sly old fox can't be trusted. A gentleman's word is sacred, but we all know Brown is not a gentleman. He has failed in business time and again. I guess this time he decided to win with no regard to honorable behavior."

"Looks like they are coming to retie us. My wrists are still rope-burned from marching tied up all day," Dan groaned as he watched Brown's men binding the hands and hobbling the feet of the Southern prisoners.

"Yes, they'll get to us in a few minutes. Looks like we're being held inside the tents where they can guard the flaps easier than having us loose. I bet Brown will claim he put us in the tents our of chivalry instead of pragmatism." As the guards got closer Pate whispered, "Stay close to me inside if you can. Old Brown isn't the only one with tricks up his sleeve–or down his boot, as the case may be."

Dan had no time to ask what the trick was before his captors reached the two men. The Northerner grabbed Dan's hands and roughly bound them together behind his back, then hobbled his feet so he could take only tottering steps. "Into the tent with you, slavers," his captors commanded.

Dan managed to follow Pate to one side near the middle of the tent. The captain sagged down there as if too weary to go all the way back. Dan sank down next to him. The rest of the prisoners flowed around them and settled down to try for a few hours' sleep. No one was in a talkative mood, so within minutes the tent was filled with snores and sounds of exhausted bodies taking their rest as best they could.

Dan lay on his side but did not sleep. Pate's comment kept him wide awake. After about an hour, the sounds outside indicated just one guard marched halfheartedly in front and one behind the prisoners' tents.

Pate whispered to Dan, "With all his gloating about capturing us and speaking directly with the Almighty, Brown made one mistake. He forgot to check my boots."

"Great! Now tell me you have a gun hidden there and I'll be a happy man." The thought of escape from this madman's clutches made Dan feel better.

"Not quite. It's where I keep my Bowie knife."

"Better than nothing, but how do we overpower two guards with one Missouri toothpick before they alert the rest of the company?"

"Ah, that would be tricky. No, the way I see it is we two just quietly escape and go for help. We should be able to catch up with Captain Woods before he reaches Lecompton. He will come back with us and release the rest of the men and take Brown into custody. The old devil took my warrant for his arrest away, but Woods knows that the warrant is real and should act on it. At least I won't have to go back and write that when I went to take Old Brown, he took me instead."

"It's a long shot but worth a try. What do you need me to do?" Dan replied.

"The knife is in my left boot on the inside. I can't reach it, but if you turn over and scoot down, you should be able to get your hands inside the boot and get it."

Dan did as Pate suggested and could feel the rough leather surface of the boot. He touched the tip of the hilt with his extended fingers, but the boot fit Pate's calf closely and Dan could not get his two bound hands inside no matter how he strained. "Maybe if you raise your feet the knife will slide out," he suggested.

Pate complied and stretched his legs as high in the air as he could while Dan, on his knees, tried to nudge the blade downward. "Hurry up," Pate whispered. "My legs are cramping."

Sure enough, encouraged my Dan's probing fingers, the hilt dropped far enough for Dan to get a grip between his two closely bound hands. "I've got it," he whispered triumphantly. "Now, just work your hands down near the blade, and I'll try and cut the rope without slitting your wrists."

"Did you have to mention that possibility? Now I'll be trembling the whole time you try and cut the bonds. I'll be picturing me gushing blood while waiting for our friend, John Brown, to come staunch the bleeding."

Dan couldn't suppress a smile. "He'd probably have to ask the Lord if it was His will that a worthless slaver bled to death."

"Not funny," Pate replied. "One time back on my parents' plantation in Virginia, one of our slaves, Apollo, slashed his wrist with a tobacco knife while harvesting. I held my shirt over the gash and tried to stop the bleeding, but I couldn't save him. He died in my arms. I cried like a baby. I wanted my dad to bury him in our family plot, but naturally they put him over on the slaves' side. Don't ever kid about a slashed wrist to me."

"Sorry. I promise to be careful." Dan thought of André and wondered if he would live to see his brother again. Unbidden thoughts of Becky crept in. If he died before he could make love to her, that would be a true tragedy. He worked slowly with the blade awkwardly clutched between his hands. *No time for thoughts of Becky now. Escape, not death, is on the agenda.* "Got it!" Dan exclaimed as the last strands parted. "Now you can cut loose your feet and me. Then we run for it." He passed the knife into his commander's hands.

Pate leaned down and slashed the rope between his feet. He then began working to free Dan's hands.

At that moment one of the sleeping militiamen cried out in his sleep. It wasn't a loud cry, but it was enough. The guard was through the door in an instant with John Brown just behind him.

Brown grabbed Pate and tossed him to the ground like a discarded apple. The knife in his hand flew upward and landed just in front of Dan's newly freed hands.

Dan lunged for the weapon and struck toward Brown's exposed chest. The guard's hand snaked forward and grabbed Dan's wrist. He forced the blade away from the Free-State leader's body.

Dan was younger and perhaps stronger, but his bound feet proved his undoing. The guard swung around and wrested the knife away. He lunged forward toward Dan's heart. Dan tried to swivel and grab the knife, but, unable to step forward freely, he toppled against his opponent. Both men went down. The guard with his arm twisted was on top.

The knife sank bone deep into Dan's thigh. The pain was sharp and intense. He heard someone screaming and realized the sound ripped from his own throat. He tried to withdraw the blade, but his bound hands were blood-soaked and he could not get a grip.

Ever so slowly, John Brown reached for the knife and withdrew it. He held it poised inches from Dan's throat. The fanatical eyes seemed to stare deep into Dan's soul. Then Brown picked up the sheath from the ground and placed the knife in it and tucked it into his belt. He pulled a dirty bandanna from the back pocket of his trousers and bound it tightly around the wound. "I saved your life, boy. Now you owe me."

"Sir, every Southern gentleman learned manners at his mammy's knee, so I will say thank you for saving my life. But life without honor is a poor thing indeed. I am sworn to avenge my friends' death at your hands. Another time and place perhaps I will challenge you to a duel." This said, Dan promptly fell to the ground in a dead faint.

Chapter 7

June 3, 1856—Middle Ottawa Creek, Kansas Territory

D an opened his eyes slowly. *I'm still alive. That leg hurts too bad to be dead.* Brown's troops were passing out a few crusts of bread for breakfast and exhorting the prisoners to get on their feet. Dan tried to rise, but the pain in his leg was too much. He cried out and fell back to the floor of the tent where he had spent the night in a pool of his own blood.

Pate reached out his bound hands to try and assist but could do little except offer moral support until Brockett hobbled over. With Brockett on one side and Pate on the other, Dan was able to stand. His own hands had been left unbound. Brown probably realized he was in no condition to escape. A feeling of vertigo had him swaying and weak.

Brockett steadied Dan. "Easy, Fitzgerald. You've lost a lot of blood."

"My fault entirely. It was a foolhardy plan doomed from the start," Pate observed.

Dan was feeling a little more normal by now. "It was a worthy try, sir. Had that soldier not cried out, it could have worked."

The rest of the prisoners in the tent had gathered around by now and were offering their sympathy.

"Brown can't keep us forever," one man muttered.

"Well, he has us for now. We'll just have to bide our time and await rescue," Pate said.

They didn't have long to wait. On the morning of June 5th, Dan was seated in front of the tent. Brocket splashed a few dribbles of water on Dan's outstretched leg, washing the wound using a small jug of water provided by their captors. Brown allowed Dan and some of the men to have their hands untied while they remained in view of the guards.

The sound of a large group of horsemen approaching the camp at a fast gallop caused the two men to exchange hopeful glances. That hope blossomed into relief when a detachment of U.S. Army Cavalry galloped into camp.

John Brown stepped out of his tent to meet the approaching soldiers. Henry Clay Pate, hands still bound, stepped from the prisoners' tent. The cavalry commander's piercing blue eyes took in the situation with a scathing glance. He appeared older than John Brown with his short, gray beard, and he had a dignity that left no doubt of his authority. "Are you John Brown of Osawatomie?"

"I am," Brown replied. "I am in command…"

At the same moment Pate rushed toward the officer. "Thank goodness, sir. This madman…"

The officer silenced both men with an upraised hand. "I am Colonel Edwin V. Sumner, United States Army commander at Fort Leavenworth, and *I* am in command here now." His deep rolling voice left no doubt he meant what he said.

Dan recalled hearing that the Colonel's nickname was "Bull Head," and now he understood why.

"Lieutenant," Sumner addressed his aide, a flamboyant young man a few years older than Dan sporting a luxurious moustache, a full black beard and a yellow sash, "see to the release of Mr. Brown's prisoners."

"Yes, sir." The lieutenant saluted smartly and dismounted in one fluid motion. He indicated to several of the cavalrymen behind him to dismount and assist with the prisoners.

The lieutenant freed Pate's bonds, then turned to Brockett and Dan."Any reason why you two are not bound?"

Dan spoke up. "I was wounded, sir, and Lieutenant Brockett is helping treat the wound."

"Let me see that." The young officer squatted down in the place Brockett vacated. He peered at the gash on Dan's leg. "It looks like it is beginning to fester. How did it happen?"

Dan explained the aborted escape attempt. He finished with his most pressing thought. "I just want to see this maniac arrested for his brutal murders and then go home to my wife."

"You live in Kansas, or are you one of these Missouri boys?"

"I have a place on Pottawatomie Creek. Right next to the Doyles' place. They helped me build my cabin." Dan didn't need to explain any further.

"Yes. Nasty business, but we are not ordered to take any action on that."

"Captain Pate had a warrant to arrest Brown," Dan insisted.

"*Had* is the factor here. I'll bet he no longer has it, right?"

"No, of course Brown took it as soon as he captured us."

"Well, without a warrant, Col. Sumner can't act. Our job is to disperse any out-of-state militia and try and maintain peace in this powder keg."

"But…" Dan tried to continue the argument.

"Just last night," the lieutenant continued, "we had to ride to Franklin. Another fracas broke out there. Some Free-Staters from Lawrence attacked Franklin trying to take back their cannon. Damned fools in Franklin loaded the thing up with nails and pieces of scrap since they had no ammunition and fired it point blank at the bunch from Lawrence. Unbelievable that no one was killed. The Free-Staters took some of Major Buford's provisions and some Sharp's Rifles stored there and fled. They managed to wound three Pro-South men. But it was all over by the time we arrived."

"This mess is not going to end easily." Dan winced as the other man probed the swollen, red cut on Dan's leg. "Ouch. It's funny going through the whole battle and not getting a scratch, then getting this just trying to get loose."

"This can kill just as easily as a bullet and a lot more painfully. You need a real doctor, but for now I have a little frontier medicine that might help." The lieutenant took a small, brown flask from his pocket. "This is pure hooch and is going to burn like fire, but it might keep your leg attached to your body."

Dan shrugged. "Have at it. I really am rather attached to my leg and would like to keep it right where it is." He gritted his teeth and omitted a low moan as the clear liquid flowed over the gash.

"Yeah. I know how it feels," the young officer commiserated. "It feels better going down the hatch!"

"Thanks. I owe you one. Maybe one day we can share a few glasses of a more civilized version of that stuff. It'll be my pleasure to buy you a round." Dan reached down and blotted the wound with his none-too-clean handkerchief. "I'm Daniel Kerry Fitzgerald originally from Louisiana, by the way."

"James Ewell Brown *Stuart from Virginia. My friends call me Jeb. Maybe one day I'll take you up on that drink.*" He gestured toward his commander who seemed to be telling the two angry opposing commanders where to go. "Looks like Colonel Sumner is going to officially send you boys home."

The colonel's voice boomed over the other camp noises. "… and you, Mr. Pate, go back to Missouri and stick to writing about military matters. Brown's sons will be freed. Until he is proven guilty, he is also free to go back to Osawatomie, and hopefully I won't ever have to deal with either of you boys again."

Stuart grinned at Dan. "I have a feeling the commander is wrong and we will be seeing a lot of both of the two militia commanders. Hope your leg is healed next time we meet." The young lieutenant returned to his horse and with a final smile rode over to join his commander.

Dan was left to contemplate how to make it back home to Becky with his throbbing wound. The angry red streaks starting to mark his injured leg made him wonder if he would even make it home again.

Chapter 8

June 6, 1856—Pottawatomie Creek, Kansas Territory

André awoke in a sweat. He had dreamed again of Dan. Not the cheerful vibrant friend and half-brother he knew but a wraith-like figure that drifted in and out of consciousness and alternatively mumbled incoherently and screamed in agony.

He rolled out of his bedroll and crossed the cabin to where he had stored a bucket of water. A dipperful later, he tried to dismiss the dream as just that, a dream with no ties to reality. Of course it was natural to have this kind of dream. Dan should have been back by now. Word had filtered back that the fighting was over. Colonel Sumner had forced Old Brown to release his prisoners.

Just a dream, André repeated. His rational mind knew that is all it was, just a product of worrying about Dan exposed to danger way too young. André knew that the young think themselves invincible. Negro men learned young they were not, but it took a little longer for that fact to invade the minds of young white males.

Warring with his rational mind were the beliefs he had learned at his mother's knee. Elise had been a practitioner of the ancient religion of Voodoo. She firmly believed dreams were an omen. Sometimes a window into the future. It's hard to shake loose your earliest beliefs.

I need to go hunting. That will take my mind off all these morbid things. Dan is fine, just delayed. He'd stop by the Doyles' cabin and let Becky know. Besides, if Dan really was wounded, nothing healed the body and spirit like some venison stew. He wondered idly if Boston girls knew how to make venison stew, but since he knew and could teach her, it made no difference. He had to admit that for a Northern woman, Becky was doing all right. She had gotten past that point of treating him like some dangerous animal she wanted to rescue but was scared he would attack her if given a chance. They had come to be friends in the past few days bound by a common worry for Dan.

Treading lightly through the woods, André felt better. He had bagged a few rabbits and a nice sized turkey. They would not go hungry.

He had been following some deer tracks when he saw a man's rough shoe print cross the path. The prints were huge, and he could not place any man nearby who should have that big a foot. He began tracking the human print. It led toward a creek which was pretty overgrown. When he reached the clearing he stopped and looked around, slowly letting his eyes drift and just scan the woods for anything unusual. It worked. He detected a flash of red low in the brush between himself and the creek. He began walking toward the unnatural color. Closer to the supposedly impenetrable brush he saw where a few vines had been woven across a hardly discernable path. Carefully he unwound the vines to allow entrance. Before he removed the last, a large figure burst forth to block his way.

The man was tall, at least six and a half feet, and proportionately broad. He must have weighed at least three hundred pounds. His skin was so black it looked almost blue in the filtered sunlight. In his right hand he held a knurled oak branch about as thick as André's thigh. "Yo' don wan' go no farther in dem 'oods." At first André thought he was speaking a foreign language until he recalled a slave he had met who spoke this dialect. "I mean you no harm." André kept the gun carefully pointed at the ground.

The giant remained in his path. He was looking at André's gun and game in a puzzled way. "Only de buckruh dey hunt tuckrey."

André realized that this man had probably never seen a Negro man with a gun in his hands. He slowly leaned his gun against a tree trunk. "I ain't a white *buckruh,* but I am a free man and I hunt what I please."

The man scratched his head. Apparently his brain size did not match his body size. "Doc, yo' gwine com' he'p me wit dis heah man," he called over his shoulder.

Within seconds, the giant was joined by a diminutive man. "Big Buhbuh becomes confused when confronted by an anomaly. He's from the low-country of South Carolina where they speak a mixture of English combined with African dialect, called Geeche or Gullah." The small man extended his hand. "I'm Harry McMullen, known as 'Doc' because while enslaved I was the property and esteemed assistant of Doctor James McMullen. Had my former master lived, I would not find myself in the forest accompanying these people."

André shook hands with Doc. If the giant's dialect was strange, the little man's perfect English was also as confusing. André realized he had stumbled across some sort of way station on the Underground Railroad. "How many of you are hiding out here?" he asked.

"Enough" was the enigmatic reply.

André recognized the reply for what it was, a clumsy attempt to appear in control while in fact these people were adrift in a strange land awaiting a stranger to lead them into a strange new lifestyle, freedom. Stories of the Underground Railroad had been whispered about even on a plantation like Irish Luck where slaves were treated well. It was every slave's favorite dream and worst nightmare. If things went well, you would be free. If just one thing went wrong, you would be dead or mutilated and returned to slavery. No one could decide which of those two was the worse fate.

"Look, I want to help. Do you need anything?" André reassured the little man. The big one was still staring and gripping his makeshift club but taking his cue from his smaller companion.

Doc's eyes drifted to the turkey slung around André's waist. "We could use some food."

André untied the turkey and a couple of the rabbits. "Do you have any way to cook these?"

Big Buhbah looked hungrily at the meat but shook his head. "We ent s'pose to mak no fiah."

André was even more confused, Doc translated. "He said, 'We're not supposed to make a fire.'" He shrugged. "It is too easily spotted, but our conductor seems to have been detained, and we used our provisions. We need to use common sense. We have to eat. Especially Renee."

"Who is Renee and why does she need to eat more than the rest of you?" André was becoming more confused as the conversation progressed.

"Maybe you had better come see for yourself." With a wave of his hand, Doc motioned Big Buhbuh to step aside and let André follow them down the path.

The narrow path wound several hundred feet and ended at the entrance to cave. The mouth was small, and André had to crawl through on his hands and knees. He was amazed that Big Buhbuh even fit through the opening, but the big man entered behind him still clutching the makeshift club. André had left his rifle sitting outside the entrance. Considering their isolation and the big man's reluctance to part with his weapon, he had some misgivings about that.

All misgivings faded as he looked at the other occupants of the small cave. Two women around his mother's age, one large and the other wizened, bent over a bed made of leaves and branches piled to raise the occupant above the damp cave floor. It was her face, seen in profile as the girl lay on her stomach that drew his attention first. It was the most perfectly sculptured face André had ever seen. As his eyes moved away from the face to the body, he gasped in anger and shock. The emaciated body seemed to belong to a twelve or thirteen-year old. Bare to the waist, Renee was covered with red ugly wounds. The kind of cuts made by a brutal lash wielded by a cruel master. The cuts crossed and crisscrossed the entire back and apparently continued beneath where the ragged blanket covered her lower back. Even as André stared in horror, the girl twisted and moaned. He caught sight of a small but well-formed breast. *Perhaps she is a bit older than I first thought. How could anyone do this to her?* After living as a slave for most of his twenty-four years, he had heard of enough cruelty to make him believe there were no depths to which some people would stoop. He might have been treated well, but Louisiana had some very harsh laws about slaves.

"André, meet Betsy," Doc gestured to the larger woman, "and Annie." He gestured to the smaller woman. He then looked down at the tormented figure on the makeshift bed. "That's Renee. I've been treating the cuts with spider webs and honey and a few herbs I carry with me. As you can see, we have all the spider webs I need. It's honey I lack. We've tried to follow a few bees back to a hive but haven't had much luck. I am afraid she is going to die."

"No!" André had seen death before, but somehow this was worse. "We have honey back at the cabins. I'll bring you a jar. I'll take these and cook them for you while I'm there. There is still plenty enough daylight to do that and make it back here."

André crawled back though the opening to daylight. He turned to Doc who had followed him out. "Can any of you use a rifle? I can leave it with you just in case."

"No, none of us have ever touched a gun. Just hurry with the honey and the food. We haven't eaten anything in days except for a few scrubby apples Big Buhbuh found on a tree near here."

"I'll be back fast as I can. By the way, who is this conductor you're waiting for?"

"His name is Mister John Brown. That is all I know about him. He is supposed to be very dedicated, so I can't figure why he is late."

"John Brown? I think you won't have to wait much longer. He was involved in some fighting, but that is all finished now so he should be along soon. If he gets here before I get back, tell him to wait for me to bring you the food and honey. I won't be long."

"Even if he does arrive we won't likely leave before dark. We always travel after dark. André." Doc hesitated.

"What is it?" André asked.

"I've been wondering about freedom. How long have you been free? Did you feel different after?"

André recalled that glorious moment in the New Orleans notary's office when Dan handed him the manumission paper that granted him his freedom. "I haven't been free for too long. I still remember the exact moment. What that notary looked like. Just how his desk was arranged. Dan's happy grin as he handed me the paper. I had a good life before. I always had a full belly, clothes and a solid roof over my head. I was given an education. I suppose in his own way, my … master cared about me. I didn't work as hard then as I do now. But, yes, freedom even when you work like a dog beats the hell out being a slave with the easiest job in the best home on earth."

André noted the tears in the eyes of the little man. "Thanks, André. I had it good too. My master always promised me I would be free when he died. He would have done it before, but he was afraid I would go off and not be able to make it by myself. He said he wanted me to know all about being a doctor even if I could not go to medical school."

"What happened," André asked.

"You mean after he died? His nephew came in and took over. Destroyed the will that said I was to be free. There was a good sum of money involved that Dr. Turner left to me. After the will was burned, everything went to the nephew. Me included. Naturally I ran first chance I got. Lucked out and made it to this Quaker preacher's house everybody said was with the Underground Railroad. So here I am. Just hoping to make it to Canada and freedom."

"You will make it. Just keep believing." André turned and headed toward home. His step was lighter than it had been since he arrived in Kansas. He was finally going to help some of his people. Doc would make it fine in Canada. He wondered what would happen to Big Buhbuh. Could he survive freedom? Well, he deserved a chance to find out. The two women probably could get jobs as cooks in Canada. And Renee? What was the fate of that poor misused scrap of humanity? Could she even survive the hard journey that lay between here and Canada?

His thoughts were still on the beautiful bronze woman-child who lay on a pain-racked bed in a damp cave. She would become a beautiful woman. If she lived to make it to Canada, she would survive. Beautiful women of any race always had a good arsenal of weapons with which to protect themselves.

When he stepped into the clearing around Becky and Dan's cabin he saw a wagon with Chieftain tied behind it in front of the cabin. André broke into a run. This morning's dream returned with crystal clarity. Dan had to be okay. He didn't like that wagon with the horse tied in back. Not one bit.

 Chapter 9

June 6, 1856—Pottawatomie Creek, Kansas Territory

André arrived at the cabin porch just as Reverend White descended the steps and began untying Dan's palomino. "Is Dan injured? Is he at least alive?" André shouted.

The preacher merely gave him a scornful look and continued conversing with Becky. "I did all I could for your husband's wound. I fear it was not enough. I am sorry." He continued to tie the horse to the porch rail.

It was too much for André. He was used to being treated as if he were a horse or expensive piece of furniture with no understanding or feelings. He could stand the insult to his person, but he had to know how Dan was. He pushed past the stunned preacher and stepped around Becky into the cabin. From the bedroom, he heard a moan. *At least he is alive!*

Dan lay on the bed, his leg swathed in a white bandage from his thigh to his knee. He was unresponsive to André's touch, and only the rise and fall of his chest indicated he was alive. Conversation from outside drifted through the open window. "Ma'am you need to teach that boy some manners. Nigras don't treat white men like that where I come from. Why, if I didn't know you and Daniel needed him for the farm, I'd string him up myself!"

Becky's tone was sharp as she replied, "Sir, André is a free man. He is our friend."

"*Friend*? Hummph," White's expression said what he thought of white people having Negro friends. "I'd best be going. I am chaplain for the Lecompton Legislature. We will see to some legislation about *friends* like that being banned from Kansas when it is a state. Even most of the Free-Staters agree on that point." He handed Becky Dan's rifle and stepped up on the wagon seat.

André heard the wagon pull away and Becky's soft step as she entered the bedroom. Together they surveyed Dan's sleeping form. Becky broke the silence. "Rev. White says Dan was stabbed while a captive and the wound is becoming gangrenous. He said he stopped at a friend's home and tried to clean and bandage it again, but it doesn't seem to be improving. He borrowed the wagon to bring Dan home to die." Her voice broke into a sob.

"He's not going to die. We'll make him better. Whatever it takes." André stooped and began unwinding the bloody bandage to reveal an angry red and blackened gash. It was oozing pus and smelled awful.

"He needs a doctor quickly. One of us is going to have to go get one. Probably the nearest is in Lane City." Becky's voice drew André's eyes from the inflamed wound.

"Stay with him. I know where to find a doctor much quicker than that." André paused in the kitchen only long enough to grab a jar of honey and a few strips of venison jerky. "By the way, I dropped some game I caught in the front yard when I saw that wagon with Dan's horse tied behind. I thought...." He didn't need to finish the sentence. He knew Becky understood what he had thought.

She nodded. "I'll get the meat in and dress it as soon as I make Dan more comfortable. Not much I can do for him beyond that. Are you sure you know a doctor nearby?" The puzzlement showed in her face, but André didn't have time to explain. He needed to get help for Dan, and Doc had said Renee needed that honey although André didn't understand why.

━━━◇━━━

Doc listened to André's hurried explanation then handed the honey to the smaller woman with a cryptic "Go ahead and apply it." To André, he stated, "Let's go."

With Doc mounted behind him on Chieftain, they made it back to the cabin in just a few minutes. Becky accepted the appearance of a strange Negro man without any comment. Maybe she realized Dan was in such a bad shape, help from any quarter was not to be scorned.

Doc studied the inflamed wound for just a few moments. He straightened and looked from André to Becky. "I won't lie to you. This man will most likely die. His odds are not good when a wound had gotten this bad."

Becky covered her face with her hands and began to sob. André shook his head. "No!" he mouthed silently.

"I said 'most likely,' not positively," Doc continued as if there had been no interruption. With both sets of eyes meeting his, Doc presented the choices. "My master, Doc Mac, was a good Christian man, but he came from a people he called 'Celts.' These people had an earlier religion based on nature. They believed that Nature, a sort of female God, wanted people to be healthy and provided many strange natural things that would cure better than scientifically created medicines. Doc Mac believed that a God, even a strange lady God, might be smarter than the doctors who taught in medical schools."

Becky and André both nodded. They would have accepted a cure from Satan himself to get Dan back on his feet.

"There are two ways to treat this man," Doc said. "The doctors at medical schools say his leg will have to be cut off and the open wound cauterized with a red hot iron." Becky covered her mouth with a shaking hand to hold back her sobs.

"You said 'two ways,'?" André questioned.

"Yes," Doc replied. "That gangrene got there because dirt got into your friend's wound. Nature provides a way to remove what is causing the problem. I must fill the wound with maggots. It is not a pretty sight."

To André's way of thinking, these were not good choices. But they did offer a glimmer of hope. "Neither is a young man with a missing leg,"

"True." Doc nodded his head slowly. "I cannot promise either way will save him. It must be your choice. If he does not make it, I do not want the choice on my soul. Either way, I will do my best for him."

André looked at Becky, whose face paled, and she swayed as though near collapse. The choice would have to be his. He tried to put himself in Dan's place. What would Danny do if he could choose? He tried to picture exuberant young Danny with only one leg. Saw him as an old man hobbling on a crutch. He knew there was really no choice. "Go with nature's way. Dan would never want to live as a cripple. But, Doc, do your very best. He means more to me than any man on earth."

Doc looked as if he read André's soul. "I will do my best for your *friend*."

If Becky noticed the emphasis, she made no mention. Just a murmured "Thank you."

André glanced from the prone form on the bed to the small dark man. "What do you need?"

"Do you have any rotting meat? I need the maggots."

André and Becky both looked at Doc helplessly. Becky recovered first. She apparently was accepting the man on face value. "There is an old bone I gave Mason and Dixon a few days ago. If they didn't finish eating it, there will be maggots on it by now. I know where they usually bury their special treats."

André knew too. "I'll go see if it is still under that old apple tree."

Doc turned back to Becky. "I need some soft material, preferably muslin or loose woven cotton, torn into wide strips."

"I have just the thing." Becky stepped to a hanger and took down a wide muslin petticoat abandoned by Mrs. Doyle and began tearing off the layers of ruffles at the bottom. By the time André returned, there was a good sized pile of white muslin, soft from years of wear.

Doc accepted the bone with its scraps of rotting meat that André presented and surveyed the infestation of crawling fly larva. "Good." He scraped off a handful of the insects and handed the bone back to André." Keep this where you can get it again."

Touching the smelly, half-eaten bone gingerly, André placed it in a wooden bowl on the mantelpiece. Meantime, Doc began placing the wriggling worm-like larva on Dan's open wound. He put them right in the midst of the worst inflammation where the wound oozed yellow pus. It was all André could do to look at it without his stomach rejecting what he had eaten earlier. Becky seemed to have regained her strength and was handing Doc the muslin strips which he bound in two or three layers loosely around the entire leg. The thought of those insects inside the bandage bothered André more than he could say. He forced out the words his mind kept repeating. "How can dirty bugs help heal Dan?"

"Nature has a use for all her creatures. Maggots eat dead meat. It's the dead meat that is killing Dan. The maggots will eat only the dead meat and leave the new healthy flesh nature is trying to form to heal him. Since the maggots are living breathing creatures, they must have air, thus the loose muslin bandages. Also because they mature and become flies, they must be removed and replaced with new fresh maggots every two days until the flesh is all clean and pink. You should see results in two or three days."

Becky nodded, and André swallowed the lump trying to rise in his throat and did likewise. He understood now why the maggots needed to remain at hand in that bowl and tried to accept Doc's view of the creatures as beneficial. His mind accepted the fact, but his stomach did not give in as easily.

Doc passed a hand over his eyes as if to rub away his tiredness. "When the wound is clean and pink, then you cover it with a coating of honey and bandage it. Change the bandages every day, and if you see any sign of redness or pus, return to using the maggots. I cannot promise anything, but it is as good if not better a chance than amputating the leg." Doc dug into his coat pocket and came out with a small leather pouch. He handed the pouch to André as if it were gold. "Also give him a spoonful of this powder mixed in water twice a day. It is made from willow bark and a few herbs and will make him sleep more deeply. The body heals better in sleep."

André shuddered. Considered in that light, he could grow to like maggots…almost.

Doc sank into a nearby chair, and André realized his weariness must be of both body and soul. Doc's future could go well or very badly. The man looked from André to the pile of muslin strips. "Would it be possible for me to take some of those strips back to bandage Renee? They are so much softer than what we have been using."

Knowing Becky would have no objections, André gathered up a handful of the muslin and placed it in Doc's bag. "I hope it helps."

Meantime, Becky had gone to the kitchen and returned with a cup of water for the exhausted old man and a canvas bag which, judging from the smell, contained some cooked rabbit. "Thank you," she said as she pressed the food into Doc's hands. "Do you want to stay here tonight, or must André bring you back to...?" She paused and André realized she had no idea where this man had come from.

"Thank you, Ma'am, but I must go back. Mister John Brown is coming any time now, and I must be there or..." He let the sentence trail, but André knew Becky understood who and what Harold McMullen was, a runaway slave waiting on the Underground Railroad connection to gain his freedom.

At the mention of "John Brown," Dan's eyelids fluttered and he seemed to be trying to speak, but the effort was too much of him. Or maybe André just imagined it.

"Come on, Doc. I'll take you back now." André helped the little man onto Chieftain and rode back to the cave not knowing what would await them there.

 Chapter 10

June 6, 1856—Pottawatomie Creek, Kansas Territory

Back at the cave, Doc slipped off the horse before André could dismount and help him. André removed Doc's bag from the saddlebag. Before he could place it in the older man's hand, a gruff voice spoke from the darkness of the brush surrounding the cave. "Put your hands in the air and turn around."

André looked to Doc for an explanation, but the old man just shrugged his puzzlement. When both men complied, a dark figure stepped from the brush. André had never met John Brown, but even without the knowledge that Brown was expected, he would have known who this man was instantly. The wild looking eyes and the unkempt hair was a dead giveaway.

John Brown addressed Doc, but he never took his eyes off André. "Who is he? You were told not to make any contact with anyone other than your conductors on the railroad!"

Doc was unperturbed. "I assume you are Mister John Brown?"

"I am! And you are endangering this entire station by mingling with this man."

"I am sorry, sir, but he discovered us and offered help. We had no food. He provided us with supplies." Doc held aloft the bag of meat.

André noted Doc didn't mention treating Dan. Perhaps he understood Brown better than André would have believed on first meeting the unimposing little man.

"Nevertheless," Brown finally took his eyes off André and fixed their steely glare on Doc, "he could betray you by accident if not deliberately. It is a breach of the rules."

"Sir, I would stake my life he will not," Doc replied.

"Yes, you will do just that. Your life, my life and the lives of your fellow passengers in there." Brown gestured toward the cave mouth.

Brown seemed to drop the subject of André as suddenly as he had raised it. "There is another problem here. That girl. She cannot go with us. It's too dangerous. She won't make it alive anyway."

"She has nowhere else to go. She has to escape. You see her back. If her owner gets her returned to him, what do you think will happen to her?" Doc straightened his posture and dropped all hint of subservience.

André's respect for the older man increased even more. The man was ready to drop with exhaustion and hunger, but he was willing to fight like a trooper for a person under his care. And not against just anyone. An armed white man who was here to lead him to freedom. Truly admirable. Truly foolish. André wondered if he could be so noble under similar conditions.

Brown's tone softened. "It's not just her condition. Where we are going, this route is dangerous. Federal troops will be very near. When I give a signal, we need to maintain total silence. Not a word. Not a movement. One cracked twig, one whisper can give us away. The girl is delirious. I watched her moaning and crying out. She cannot go with us. For all our sakes."

"But..."

"I'm sorry. I have vowed to help all my Negro brethren escape the terrible bondage of slavery. My life is devoted to that end. But better one girl than all of us." Brown's fiery eyes held a hint of compassion.

André realized the complexity of this man's character. Brown would kill innocent people without batting an eye. He would lead men into battle for his beliefs, but he was truly sorry to sacrifice one young girl for the safety of the group. *What a strange and confused man.* André spoke up. "I'll take her with me and keep her safe until she can travel."*My God! I've just made a decision for the first time without consulting Dan that risks his life and Becky's as well as my own hide.* It dawned on André for the first time. *This is one of the things freedom means. Responsibility. For yourself and others.*

Brown and Doc both stared at him. After a moment Doc nodded his consent. Brown spoke. "You realize what risk you take. You could be killed or imprisoned. If a slave catcher finds her with you, you could be dragged back into slavery –I assume you are a freedman. "

André nodded. Suddenly he wanted to do this. He hated risking Dan and Becky's lives, but he knew both would agree in a second. "Tell me how to treat the wounds. There's a woman back at the cabin." Neither André nor Doc indicated by word or look that that woman was a white woman married to a Southerner currently injured in a fight against John Brown's militia. Life was strange sometimes.

Brown nodded his acceptance. He called to the two women in the cave to prepare the girl for travel. Doc quickly gave André instructions for Renee's care.

Doc and André shook hands as Brown's group prepared to leave. "Take care, Doc. If anybody deserves freedom, it's you," André said. "I'll do my best for Renee, and when she is better I'll get her to Lawrence. There are people there who will help her get to Canada."

As André settled the injured girl into the saddle in front of him, he looked back at the ragged line of people already melting into the shadows. He found himself doing something he didn't do often, praying.

Chapter 11

June 6, 1856—Pottawatomie Creek, Kansas Territory

Becky felt helpless as she dabbed a damp cloth over Dan's forehead. He had regained consciousness if not lucidity a few moments ago. The way he thrashed around, she was afraid he would undo his bandage. He alternately mumbled and shouted. The angry shouts seemed to be directed toward his father. The tone and words he used were shocking. When he switched to the mumbled words, they were more plaintive and sad. He called out for André mostly. Then his voice seemed to drip sadness when he called out to people called Colette, Elise and Sallie. From his mumblings she gleaned that Colette was his mother and she had died recently. Who Elise and Sallie were was a complete mystery. Then he called out "my brother." She hadn't known he had a brother, but then she really knew so little about him.

She spoke to him softly. Meaningless words just to let him know he was not alone and was going to get better, but she wasn't sure her voice could reach him in the desolate place his soul seemed to have drifted into. Finally he lapsed into a calmer sleep and Becky was once more alone for all practical purposes. She began to drift toward sleep as she realized André seemed to be taking a long time. Suddenly she sat bolt upright. Totally awake. Dan's mumblings made more sense in light of a lot of things she had half noticed. The closeness between Dan and André. The way he had never mentioned his father to her when she told him of her father's illness and death on the long ride back from Lawrence. Finally the striking resemblance between the two men. Had André not been darker, she would have seen it at first meeting.

André was Dan's brother! Now Becky understood the anger Dan seemed to have for his father. She had often heard speeches by abolitionists condemning this part of slavery as particularly vile but had never thought of the logical consequences. Dan had been forced to face those consequences in his own life. He had not come to Kansas Territory so much as run away from unpleasant facts he must have recently learned about his father. That explained his freeing of André and his dislike of slavery in spite of his Southern upbringing.

It was already dawn. Perhaps André had gone directly to his own cabin, but Becky doubted that. He was too worried about Dan not to return here. She decided a cup of mulled apple cider would help soothe her frazzled nerves. About the time she had lit a small fire to heat the cider, she heard a horse outside. André probably had returned at last. She added an extra portion of the cider. He would need some also.

But when she opened the door, she was thrown into shock again. André was gently carrying what appeared to be a sleeping girl. He stood undecidedly on the stoop. "I have a problem. This girl… She is one of the runaways and …." He appeared uncertain of his welcome.

"Well, bring her in." Becky opened the door wider.

André still hesitated. "She is injured and needs care."

"All the more reason to bring her in. I've made up a pallet next to the bed for me to sleep near Dan, but put her there. I can make up another for me." Becky led into the bedroom.

"And Dan? Any change?" André asked as he laid down his burden as easily as possible.

"He regained consciousness but was just rambling. He didn't seem aware of where he was or who I am," Becky replied.

The girl whimpered when her body made contact with the blanket. She looked up and saw Becky first. She seemed to be about to bolt from the cabin until her eyes rested on André. Then she sighed and closed her eyes and laid her head back on the soft blanket. Becky saw flecks of blood on the rough bandages covering the girl. "Good Heavens, what happened to her?" she asked.

André straightened and looked Becky in the eyes. "She is a runaway slave who was beaten by her former mistress. Her name is Renee. That is all I know about her. We need to talk about what we are going to do about her."

"Let's go in the kitchen. I was just warming some mulled cider," Becky replied. "As for the girl, we will just nurse her along with Dan. Maybe we could open a hospital." Becky tried for a joking tone, but it fell flat.

"This is not something to be decided lightly, Becky. Do you know that besides jail time and fines under federal law, the Kansas Territory Legislature has made helping a fugitive slave punishable by death?"

"That bogus legislature!" Becky's unladylike snort showed her contempt for any laws they passed. "We will certainly help her."

"Thank you." André hadn't realized until that moment how much he was counting on her help. "I think Doc gave her a sleeping draught so she would not feel the pain of moving here by horseback. She should be conscious by morning. Maybe Dan will be awake then too. Do you want me to stay here tonight or go back to my cabin?"

"Why not just set up a pallet here in case Dan or your little Renee awakens during the night."

"She's not *my* Renee. I just want to help her to freedom."

"Yeah. Well, that look she gave you was pretty possessive," Becky tossed toward André's broad back as he began rummaging in the chest for a blanket.

 Chapter 12

June 12, 1856—Pottawatomie Creek, Kansas Territory

Dan raised his head from the pillow. The last thing he remembered was Martin White helping him into a wagon to go where. Home? Slowly, some of the immediate past came into focus. He was in the Doyle cabin. No, it was his cabin now. His and Becky's. He was a married man. He had vague recollections of Becky and André standing over him. A strange Negro man was with them. They poked and probed at his leg. His leg! That came back clearer. Someone, maybe a doctor, saying the leg needed to be amputated. *Oh my God. No! It has to be still there. It aches.* Gingerly, he lowered his arm to touch the aching limb. He remembered hearing people say an amputated limb still would hurt with something called phantom pains. He didn't breathe again until he touched solid flesh. When his fingers probed the wound it felt cooler, drier. *Could it have healed? How long have I been unconscious?* He tried to probe his faulty memory, but little came through except Becky and André tending him and talking to him. He had one clear memory of someone mentioning John Brown. He had wanted to get up and fight with Brown, but he could not. It seemed they had also talked to someone else. Who else would be here. It was too much for him and he lapsed into sleep. When he next woke everything seemed clearer.

Becky was just entering the room, and she called out, "He's awake, André! Come see!"

Dan tried to sit up and found that a bit difficult until Becky and then André rushed to aid him. Dan tried for a teasing tone, but even that came out a little off. "Waking up is not a big deal. I do it every day and never got this reaction before."

Becky burst into tears, and André swallowed a few times before he replied. "Maybe that's because you didn't wake up for the last five days. We were worried."

"Five days? I just slept for five days?"

Becky dried her eyes and sat next to him on the bed. "We were so worried. You did stir and mumble a little when we changed the maggots...."

"Maggots? Dead things get filled with maggots. My God, was I that far gone?" Dan reached down to probe the healing wound again.

"But my wound feels better."

"It was that Negro doctor, sort of doctor anyway," Becky floundered not knowing where to begin.

André took over. "Doc showed us how to put maggots on the wound to clean it."

"So I owe my leg and my life to a 'sort-of-doctor' who lets maggots eat his patients?" Dan tried to ease his fingers under the bandage just to be sure nothing was still crawling on him. Eating his infected flesh. He shivered. Still the leg seemed much improved. "Where is this medical wonder? Maggots or not, I do want to thank him."

"He's gone. He was hiding out on the Underground Railroad waiting for … for his conductor to lead him toward Canada."

"Well. I certainly hope he makes it. It seems I owe him a lot and hope one day to repay him."

André glanced across at Becky. "Well, Danny Boy, there is something you can do to repay him. How do you feel about another mouth to feed around here?"

Dan's eyes shot to Becky. Impossible. She did say he had "stirred and mumbled" but surely nothing more. He couldn't have! And it was only five days.

Becky turned red as she realized where Dan's thoughts were going. André chuckled. "Now I know you're getting better. No, you haven't been that active yet." André explained the situation with Renee to Dan and concluded with, "Becky's willing to help but I can move Renee to my cabin if you are worried about the law…."

Dan interrupted. "Certainly not. I want to help her. It's the least I can do to repay this sort-of-doctor who is responsible for my leg healing."

"I knew you would want to help. Let me go an' get the poor child and introduce you two. She's a bit skittish around white folks, so go easy. She's in the kitchen. Poor thing, her back is still sore and oozing, but she insists on helping." André turned and headed for the door. "I'll bring you back some of the venison stew she is making. It's tasty. That young 'un does know her way around a kitchen."

When André had left, Becky patted Dan's hand. "I am so glad you're getting better. A couple of things about Renee while André is gone. She is not 'skittish' about white people: She's scared to death. With good reason. She told André how she got in her condition. Her master had been raping her since she was about twelve or thirteen. Then he got killed in a duel over a horse race. She thought things might be better, but her mistress knew about what had been going on and somehow blamed Renee for seducing her husband. She put her in the kitchen doing the dirtiest jobs there and beat her for everything or nothing." Before Becky could finish the story, André returned, propelling a frightened Renee before him. "This here is Dan, and he ain't goin' to hurt yo' at'tall, lil' gal. Dan, our new house guest, Renee." He completed the strange introduction.

"Hello, Renee. Welcome to our humble cabin. As soon as I am up and about, I'll make you a proper bed. Seems you have been sleeping on a pallet on the floor." Dan noticed that the "child" seemed about sixteen or seventeen. Her skin was what Louisiana people called café au lait. He could not help but notice she was the most attractive female of any race he had seen in a long time.

Renee looked at her bare feet and mumbled, "Thankee, sir. I is fine where I is. I appreciate what you and the missus is doing fo' me." She barely raised her eyes to meet Dan's for a second and skidded them across Becky before she tried to back out of the room. "'Scuse me, master, missus, I got to get back to the kitchen and see 'bout the stew."

"No. No!" Becky cried out. "No 'master' or 'missus' here. We are your friends. We want to help you. We're just Becky and Dan."

"Yes'um, " the girl replied, her eyes still downcast. "I'd betta be goin' back to the kitchen 'fore that stew done burns."

André laid the bowl down on the table by the bed for Dan."I'll help you. That pot is too heavy for you to lift. Your cuts will open again."

"Thankee." Renee raised her head giving André a fleeting look from emerald green eyes shaded by long dark lashes.

After the two had left, Dan spoke up. "I guess the other things you were going to tell me about Renee are she is *not* a child and is already in love with André."

Becky nodded. "He doesn't see her as anything but an abused child."

Dan tackled the stew with a vengeance. "I can see my recuperation time is not going to be dull. I think André has met his match."

 Chapter 13

July 3, 1856—Kansas Territory

Dan leaned on his cane. Mason and Dixon frolicked nearby. He was feeling restless. Although his wound was healed, he still limped and could not put full weight on his right leg. Becky and André kept telling him that he needed to speak to a doctor and see if there was anything further to be done for the leg. Maybe he should, but he didn't know any doctors and hated to take time off from his farming duties. The corn the Doyles had planted was silking nicely, and it wouldn't be long to harvest time, while the crop he and André put in was just a few weeks behind. Dan looked forward to their first crop.

He planned on buying a good bull and a few head of cattle, so he would keep much of the corn for feed and next year's seed, but there should be enough to sell in town at auction for some cash money. In spite of all the feuding going on in Kansas Territory, things were looking good here.

He spotted André with Renee, tagging close behind near the cornfield. André was looking for a few early ears to have for dinner, and Renee could always be found near André. The girl was still wearing the same baggy dress left behind from Mrs. Doyle that they had put on her while her lacerated back healed and she needed loose clothing. She refused to put her old clothes back on, claiming they were "evil."

Physically, Renee had blossomed. Good food had put some much needed weight on her, and her small figure became more rounded every day. Her back was nicely healed, and André was talking about getting her into Lawrence or Topeka and set up with the Underground Railroad. Emotionally, there were still open wounds. She still cringed whenever Becky or he came near her. Naturally when they had company, she instantly melted into the brush and hid at André's cabin until it was safe. Usually she waited there until André escorted her back.

Perhaps today might be the day to go seek out a doctor. Neighbors had recommended a Dr. Miles in Topeka. Since the Free-State legislature was due to meet there tomorrow, the doctor would be in town. Word was out that the legislature had been ordered not to assemble, so Pro-Southerners and Free-Staters alike were waiting to see what happened.

André had been reminding him they needed some supplies. They could get things at better prices in Topeka. Yes. This was the right time. If they left now and camped along the road, they could be there by mid-morning.

Becky waved from the porch until the wagon turned down the road. Then she headed back to the house. It was time, long past time in fact, to speak with Renee.

"Renee, can I talk to you for a moment?"

"Yes'um." The younger woman came toward Becky. Her eyes stared intently at the planks of the floor.

"Please look at me. I want to help you, Renee, but you have to learn to trust me. I know you have been through a lot, but all white people are not alike any more than all colored people. Do you understand?"

"Yes'um." The eyes met Becky's for an instant and then gazed downward once more.

Becky sighed. "I know your secret. Will you let me help?"

"My secret? Ah don' understan' what yo' sayin'."

"It's obvious to everybody how you feel about André. Everybody but André that is."

That got attention. "Yes'um. I sure does like that man."

"I know, and I would like to help you get him to notice you that way."

"I done tried everythin', and he still thinks I's a chile."

"Maybe you haven't tried the right things."

"Wat right things? You really gonna he'p make him care fo' me?" In her excitement, Renee was actually meeting Becky's eyes.

Becky nodded. "For starters, try using more correct grammar." She amended, "speak more like he does."

"I been trying to pay attention when yo'…you and the mas… I mean Dan talk. You think I could really talk good lik' dat."

"Yes, I do, and I could also teach you to read. Would you like that?"

The girl's sparkling eyes spoke before her words confirmed it. "Oh yes'um, I'd rightly lik' dat."

Becky eyed the girl's ugly oversized dress. "First thing we need to do is get you into some more attractive clothing, and maybe a little hairstyling would help."

Becky led Renee into the bedroom. "I have some green and yellow calico I was saving to make a special dress. It will be perfect with your eyes." She gathered up her sewing kit and the material and motioned for Renee to undress so they could fit her. When the girl hesitated, Becky added. "It's okay. I know the other secret too. I watched you when you were sick those mornings. I know you're pregnant. About three months I'm guessing, right?"

Renee just nodded.

 Chapter 14

July 4, 1856—Topeka, Kansas Territory

As Dan and André neared Topeka, the road became congested. Dan nodded to a new group of riders entering the road from a side trail. "Looks like everybody is coming to see if the Free-State Legislature will dare to meet today."

"Yeah, between that little tea party you were invited to that dang near cost you a leg, then the Free-Staters attacking Franklin a coupla days later, then the Southern boys hitting Osawatomie and all, things have really been heating up. It don't look good, Danny Boy." André navigated the wagon expertly to miss a few deep ruts in the road.

"Well, it's none of our business. I would like to see John Brown at the end of a rope for what he did to the Doyles, but I've had enough of all this squabbling. I don't believe in slavery, but I am a Southerner. This whole mess needs to blow over. I just want to get a good corn harvest, and then we can invest in some cattle."

When André didn't reply, Dan studied his brother's face. "Well, what's bothering you? Come on out with it."

"Just thinking about how lucky I am to be free but sort of feeling guilty. You know what I mean? So many of my people aren't free and live terrible lives. I never thought too much about other people's troubles much before all this."

"You mean like Renee?"

"Uh huh. Renee and Doc and all the others like them."

Dan thought a minute. "I wish I could help, but what can one man do? We're just ordinary people. This is a whole way of life. Politics. Money. Society. Best to just take care of our own and try and make things work out."

"Speaking of 'things working out,' how are thing with you and Becky?" André changed the subject.

"We're friends, but I really want to make this marriage a real one, not just a marriage of convenience. I mean sleeping right next to her and not doing anything is killing me."

André laughed. "I'll bet it is. I think she really cares but is afraid to hurt your leg."

"Yeah. Well, she's hurting something else a lot worse."

"Use your charm. It always worked on them Louisiana girls, didn't it?"

"They were different. Becky is, well, she's special. And to turn the tables, what about Renee?"

"I plan to talk to a man in Topeka about helping her."

"André, that's not the help she wants from you."

"What do you mean?"

"Come on, don't you see the way she looks at you?"

André shrugged. "She's just infatuated. She's a kid. I'm the first man who has been nice to her."

"For a smart guy, you can be pretty dumb sometimes."

By now they had reached Topeka and followed the flow of traffic into town. It had been cloudy most of the morning, but now nearing mid-day, the temperature felt like it was at least 100 degrees and both men were hot and tired of watching people who seemed to have no regard for their lives and stepped right in front of the wagon. "Would you look at that. I never saw so many people in my life." The town was teeming. People had set up camp just off the street; food was roasting over dozens of campfires. Horses were picketed in every vacant space they saw. Militia wearing uniforms of white pants, blue shirts, and Kossuth hats paraded. A new American flag, with an extra star in the corner, obviously representing Kansas Territory, but not in the Union, was hoisted over Constitution Hall.

Dan pointed. "Look. There is Colonel Sumner and my old friend Lieutenant Stuart. I owe him a drink." Stuart must have seen Dan as well because he separated from the troops and approached the wagon.

"I see you managed to keep that leg attached." The young lieutenant greeted Dan.

"Yeah, no thanks to your rotgut treatment. Still I owe you one. Are you free to stop in a tavern and have a quick drink and maybe some lunch?"

"Maybe later I'll take you up on the lunch but no taverns in Topeka. Town fathers have ruled alcohol cannot be sold here. Mr. Oakley has a hotel with a fine dining room just down the street. I could meet you when all this ruckus is finished. Right now we have some business to take care of. The colonel brought me along to keep these fellows in line while we attend to business." Stuart gestured to the military band lined up ahead of three squadrons of dragoons and two loaded brass cannon.

"So you really aren't going to let the legislature meet?" Dan was impressed by all the firepower on display.

"Right. Word is the order came directly from Secretary of War Jefferson Davis. The old man is not too happy about this. You know

'Freedom of Assembly' and all that constitutional stuff. Still, orders are orders."

André spoke up. "Yeah, we do live under a constitution that guarantees some kinds of freedom to some people.."

Stuart looked sharply at André. For a moment Dan wondered if the lieutenant would take offence at a Negro man speaking up like that. Slowly, Stuart's lips turned up and he began to laugh. "In this territory, one man's freedom is stepping on another man's rights, and every mother's son is shooting at everybody else. Us poor soldier boys just try and maintain law and order."

The military band sounded a trumpet, and Stuart turned. "Duty calls. I'll be in the hotel dining room later this evening. If you get your business taken care of, I'll see you then."

André pulled the wagon to the side and tied the horses to the tiny piece of hitching post not already in use. "Let's watch the show, Danny Boy."

They watched as Colonel Sumner dismounted and walked toward the legislative hall. He was intercepted by an older lady who spoke up loudly. "We have met to present a banner to one of these Topeka companies on the day of our would-be-independence."

The Colonel was undeterred as he continued toward his mission, but he replied courteously, "Madame, I hope you will be independent."

He continued toward the legislative officer at the door of Constitution Hall. Here he proceeded to read his orders to the group assembled in the doorway of the hall. "I am called upon this day to perform the most painful duty of my whole life. Under the authority of the President's proclamation, I am here to disperse this Legislature, and therefore inform you that you cannot meet. I, therefore, order you to disperse. God knows that I have no party feeling in this matter and will hold none so long as I occupy my present position in Kansas. I have just returned from the Borders, where I have been sending home companies of Missourians, and now I am ordered here to disperse you. Such are my orders, and you must disperse. I now command you to disperse. I repeat that this is the most painful duty of my whole life."

Having delivered his ultimatum, he turned and remounted at the head of his men, obviously ready to do his duty and employ force if the demands were not met. It was equally obvious he was hoping for a peaceful end to the confrontation.

He and the crowd did not have long to wait. The Sergeant at Arms for the legislature returned in a moment and stated, "By order of the lawful acting governor of the Territory of Kansas, John Curtis, acting on the command of our *lawful* governor, Charles Robinson, currently detained *unlawfully* in prison by federal forces, this body will now disband."

Sumner chose to ignore the legality or lack of it regarding Doctor Robinson's status and signaled his men to stand at rest.

Dan and André decided to leave the wagon tied here for the time being as it would have been impossible to drive through the throng. Dan would make his way to the doctor's office. André left to meet with a contact, a John Anderson, who he had been told could help Renee on her way to freedom. They agreed to meet at Jones General Store on Kansas Street at four in the afternoon.

 Chapter 15

July 4, 1856—Topeka, Kansas, Territory

André knocked at the door at 133 Quincy Street. The door was quickly opened by an attractive young blond woman. "Yes?" she asked.

"Is this the William Scales residence?" André asked.

"Yes. I'm his daughter, Adeline. Did you need to speak to my father?"

"No, I need to see a Mr. John Armstrong."

The woman's expression changed to one of understanding. "Please come in." She swung the door wider giving André a view of a sunny parlor. "John's my fiancé. I'll get him right now."

She led André to a comfortable overstuffed chair in the parlor. Brown had only told him to contact Armstrong when Renee was well enough to travel. He didn't know what to expect from the man, but he was not expecting this cordial reception. White people did not usually invite strange Negro men into their homes. He didn't have long to ponder. A dark-haired man about André's age emerged from a rear door. He stuck out a welcoming hand to André. "John Armstrong. So glad you finally made it here."

André stared at the extended hand and then tentatively lifted his own to shake it. "André Fitzgerald, but I think you have me confused with someone else."

"Oh my. Oh yes. I was expecting someone. They told me he was a freedman and I … we all assumed…not many freedmen come here." Seeming to realize none of this was making any sense to his guest, the man started again. "Sorry. The man we were expecting is overdue and naturally when someone fitting his description arrived Addie just assumed it was that person. You are still welcome in our home in your own right, Mr. Fitzgerald. How can I help you?"

Not quite sure if this strange man would report him to the authorities, André tried to word his request carefully. "I was told you might be able to help me get a passenger connected with a certain railroad."

Armstrong hesitated several moments. "I'm sure you know no tracks have been laid into Kansas. Which line were you referring to?"

Throwing caution to the wind, André responded. "I am hiding a runaway and need help getting her to Canada." He waited. Armstrong would either send for the sheriff or reveal his involvement.

"Who told you I could help with this matter?"

"John Brown. The girl was in a group he was leading from near Pottawatomie Creek, but she was injured and could not travel then."

"I assume you are a freed man. Do you have a claim of your own near Pottawatomie Creek?" Armstrong had slipped into a nearby chair and was studying André closely.

"Yes on both counts, but what does that have to do with helping this girl to freedom?" The scrutiny was making André uneasy.

"You are correct in assuming I am part of what we call the Underground Railroad, but there is a problem. There is no one in the Pottawatomie Creek area to help as a conductor, the person who leads the slaves to the next safe house."

"I thought John Brown did that."

"He does, but lately he has gotten so busy. It's a 'too much need and not enough help' situation. We had been expecting someone from near Osawatomie who would take over that section. That is who I thought you were when you arrived."

"Does that mean no one can help Renee?" André didn't like where this was going.

"No. No. It may take some time, but we will help her." Armstrong rose. "Let me ask Mrs. Scales for some refreshment. All this confusion made me forget my manners."

He stepped back though the door to the house's interior, and André was left alone for a few moments. He knew what question was coming, so he gave it some thought. He didn't mind risking his life, but he had to consider Dan and Becky. Also he was relatively new to the area and didn't know his way around the woods like someone who had been here longer.

Armstrong returned accompanied by an older version of Adeline. She carried a tray with sandwiches and tall cool drinks. "Hello, I'm Carolyn Scales. Welcome to our home."

André accepted a sandwich and drink. "Pleased to meet you, Mrs. Scales. I'm André Fitzgerald."

She explained, "There is no alcohol as my family and I are temperate. We feel that alcohol is a demon and robs a man of his money and good sense."

André sipped from his glass. He tasted a strawberry flavor sweetened with syrup. "That's fine. This is delicious."

Carolyn Scales left André and her future son-in-law alone to talk. Armstrong didn't mince words. He got right to the subject. "You could be a godsend to us right now. All you would need to do is lead the 'passengers' from the 'station,' that cave where you met Brown, and bring them to the home of a Methodist preacher near Prairie City."

André shook his head. "I don't know. I'm new to Kansas. What about this preacher and his wife? Couldn't they pick up the runaways and take them home?"

"No, it's not right to ask more of them. He is a circuit rider around this area and uses that as cover when he brings the passengers here. These people risk a lot just opening their home to them."

"There must be someone better fitted than me," André stalled.

"Perhaps. I won't lie to you. It is dangerous as I am sure you know. But you were a slave once yourself. You know how important this work is."

André did understand but…"I've got to think about what you've told me. Meantime, what about Renee?"

"No matter your decision, we will help her. I'm afraid it will be near the end of August before we can make any arrangement. Give me directions to your claim, and I will send someone there when we are ready. Meantime, don't make any trails that lead to the cave. It's the only station around there, and we can't risk anyone finding it."

"Before you go would you like to see our safe house here? It's where Renee will be hiding while she is here."

Armstrong led André through the house. He noted it was rather large for just one family, even with a future son-in-law in residence. Noting André's expression, Armstrong explained, "The Scales take in a few boarders. It's a good cover to explain people coming and going all the time."

"Doesn't that increase the risk of exposure?" André questioned.

"Yes. But it also helps with funds which are necessary. It costs a good bit to move even one runaway from here to the next station. "Food, clothes, maintenance of horses and wagons, sometimes bribes. Then too my sister, Sarah, needs books to teach the slaves a little reading while they are here. We like to let them keep their own book when they leave."

"Isn't it risky to transport them in a wagon? What if someone sees them or the wagon breaks down?"

"Not in our wagon. No one will see them."

They had reached the cellar by this time. Armstrong opened the door; it was heavy, double barred and bolted on both sides. "That is so no boarder will wander down here. Our passengers know to keep this door locked and not open it unless they hear a special knock." He pushed open the door; it moved silently for such a large structure. "No one is here now, but if they were and heard anyone coming, they would get in here as quietly as possible."

He indicated a huge sugar hogshead near the back wall. André had seen these in Louisiana at sugar plantations, but this was the largest he had ever seen, about four foot high and over three feet in diameter at the top opening. He peered inside. There were a few blankets and some straw. Not comfortable for living in but a wonderful hiding place.

"Come on out here and look at this." Armstrong beckoned him through a small door near the rear of the room.

Both men had to duck to fit through the little opening. Parked very close to the wall of the house was a sturdy closed carriage. "It cost us over six hundred dollars to have this built."

André examined the carriage. It was sturdy and smaller inside than it appeared. It would have seated four good-sized adults inside and one or two others up front with the driver. André was not impressed. "Very nice," was the best he could truthfully muster.

Armstrong laughed. "Yeah, I know you are thinking you could buy this for four hundred any day. Look here." He reached inside and flipped back the rear seat exposing a small trap door leading to a large space between the floor of the carriage and the outside bottom. "We can hide six people in here."

André smiled. "Now I am really impressed."

The two men shook hands, with André promising to consider the possibility of actually becoming part of this Underground Railroad.

After he left, André wandered slowly back toward the general store where he would meet Dan. He felt good trusting Renee to such careful people. These white people were risking so much for strangers. Could he ever do this much good for his own people, he asked himself?

Dan left the doctor's home and headed for the Topeka House. He had not received any miracles from the doctor nor had he expected any. He had paid two dollars for the doctor to examine his leg, nod his head and tell Dan how wonderful the wound was looking. The doctor further advised regular use of the leg to strengthen it. In time, he predicted it would be almost as good as new. Well, what had Dan expected?

At the Topeka House, he saw Stuart deep in conversation with a man in his middle twenties. Whoever this person was, Dan observed he was successful, dressed in a black broadcloth frock coat, blue and red paisley waistcoat and fitted fawn-colored britches covered to the knee by a shiny pair of black riding boots. A broad brimmed planter's hat sat on the empty chair next to him.

As Dan approached, the stranger pounded the table and shouted, "Dammit, Stuart, I'm not trying to stir up trouble. These Bible-thumping

New England Yankees have no right to come into Kansas and try and change our way of life."

Stuart saw Dan approaching and rose to greet him. "Hello, Fitzgerald. Come on over and meet a fellow Southerner. Joseph Orville Shelby of Waverly, Missouri— Daniel Fitzgerald, from around Potawatomie Creek. "

The two men exchanged pleasantries, and Dan took a seat between Shelby and Stuart. Shelby continued as if there had been no interruption. "These rascals burned my sawmill. Danged thing wasn't even insured. They need to be sent scampering back up north with their mangy tails between their legs!"

"Jo, way I hear it is that was a bit of revenge for some shooting up you and your Blue Lodge boys did on the Kansas side of the line," Stuart drawled.

"Stuart, on my word of honor as a gentleman, I never shot any man who wasn't pointing a gun or knife at me first. That shooting story came about when some of us Missouri boys tried to cast our legal vote. We all staked a claim on some Kansas land. No reason I can't stake a Kansas claim and have the right to vote, is there?"

"None except you already own half of Lafayette County between your plantation and the rope factory, not to mention your steamboats and all the other pies you have a finger in." Stuart raised an eyebrow. "Part of the rule about claims is that the owner must work the claim for five years. I seriously doubt you could find time to work a Kansas claim,"

Shelby ignored the remark. "Somebody has to stop those bastards from coming down here and telling us how to run our lives. It's our business, not theirs. This isn't just about the slavery issue. It's about our rights. And we are in the right legally. That is why we organized the 'Law and Order Party,' but of course the news keeps referring to us as the 'Pro-Slavery Party' instead."

"Ah yes. But the slavery issue plays better in the press. As long as there are fire-eating abolitionists on one side and hot-heads like you on the other side, there is plenty of fuel to fan the fire," Stuart reminded him.

Shelby turned to Dan. "You are a bona-fied resident of Kansas, not one of us 'Border Ruffians,' so what is your take on the way to get rid of those Boston bastards?"

Dan thought a bit before answering. He respected both of these men as fellow Southerners, but he felt his attitude toward slavery differed from theirs. He felt his father had betrayed him as well as his mother and even Elise. He was not ashamed of André, but he couldn't admit to the world what a scoundrel his father was. "I got this limp riding with

Colonel Pate trying to apprehend John Brown after he murdered my neighbors and friends. I abhor men like that and would gladly send all of them straight to the devil instead of just chasing them back to New England. But I've seen the evils of slavery firsthand. I think it corrupts the master while demeaning the slave. I freed my man-servant before leaving Louisiana to come here."

Stuart spoke up first. "I agree our 'peculiar institution' has flaws, but remember we didn't invent the system. The Yankees are still building slave ships and bring in slaves even though it's now illegal. While I have not freed my manservant, Mulatto Bob, I think highly of him. We grew up together and played together as children. Were I to free him, he would still stay with me, I believe. I trust him with my money and my horses."

Based on his expression, Dan believed Shelby was going to violently condemn them for not being strong supporters of the slavery system. He surprised Dan when for once his answer was not contentious. "I have to say, I own a large number of slaves. I would not consider freeing them but have to admit some of them are more like friends than servants. Billy Hunter has been my personal servant since I was eleven and, like JEB, I would trust him with my money or my horses." He continued. "My cousin, Frank Blair, is running for Congress this year. He believes gradual emancipation with compensation is the answer. Frank and I don't always see eye to eye, but we are good friends in spite of our difference of opinion."

Dan was happy to realize his new acquaintance was broadminded enough to be tolerant of those with differing opinions. At least as long as they didn't try and ram those opinions down his throat.

The three men went their respective ways after the meal with no thought to possible future meetings.

Chapter 16

July 5, 1856—Pottawatomie Creek, Kansas Territory

Dan and André were both engrossed in their separate thoughts on the ride home. Conversation was sparse and inconsequential. They reached Dan's cabin just before sunset. "It sure feels good to get back home," André commented.

"You got that right," Dan agreed.

They drew the wagon to the porch, and Dan began unloading the portion of the supplies that would remain here. Becky came out to greet the men. "Where's Renee?" André asked.

"She went to your cabin. Says she is going to cook something special for supper for you."

It seemed a little strange since the four of them had been taking their meals at Dan's cabin since his injury and Renee's arrival. Still, some time alone with Renee was not unwelcome. André thought he could explain better if he were alone with the girl what would happen next in Renee's journey toward freedom. Also, he had not mentioned his discussion with Armstrong beyond telling Dan an approximate date when Renee's "conductor" would contact him. This would give him chance to consider that matter when Renee went to bed.

Before André reached his doorway, the odor of freshly baked apple pie assailed his nose. *Boy, I haven't smelled anything that good since Momma's special apple pie back at Irish Luck.* A sudden wave of nostalgia hit him. He realized he missed his family: Elise, Sallie, Mister Michael and even Miz Collette. Dan's mother had never been particularly affectionate toward him, but again she had never been unkind. He contrasted that with Renee's past history. Although Renee had no choice but to submit to her master's demands, as soon as the man was dead and buried, his wife began beating the girl unmercifully as if to punish her for something she had no control over. *Life is unfair. Especially if you are a Negro. Might as well accept that fact.*

Inside even a greater surprise awaited him. The sloppily kept interior was still poorly furnished, but every board was freshly cleaned.

Every corner was swept dust free. A clean white cloth was placed over the stump used for a table. The pie that his nose had promised him sat covered with a scrap of muslin on a clean windowsill. On the newly scrubbed hearth, a cast iron spider holding biscuits had been pulled back just far enough to remain warm. A large black pot simmered with something that smelled delicious.

The cabin was not the only thing transformed. Gone was the thin waif wearing an oversized shapeless dress in dirt brown. Presiding over this feast was a shapely young woman. Her curves were accentuated by a well-fitted calico dress of a green and yellow color that seemed to be reflected in her enormous eyes. Her gleaming black hair had been pinned up on top of her head and held in place with a tiny spray of wildflowers.

"What did you do?" Not the most flattering thing to say, André realized, but he was very confused by this new Renee. She did not fit the image he held in his mind. In fact she created some rather disturbing images in his mind. *Why haven't I seen her as a woman? She is beautiful and definitely not a child.*

Renee seemed pleased with his reaction. "Wat ya...I mean, what do you think?" She pirouetted in the first show of coquetry he had seen from her.

André was almost moved to tears. *She is trying so hard to please me. Even trying to talk better. My God, I've been a blind fool.* He answered through the lump in his throat "You look lovely. The cabin has never looked so good, and that smell is driving me crazy. When can we eat?"

Renee looked disappointed that he didn't take her in his arms, but he needed some thinking time. *Was this what Becky and Dan had seen all along. A beautiful woman completely in love with him. Him! André!* It would be so easy to respond naturally, but he needed to think of her safety first. As a runaway, she was far safer in Canada than Kansas Territory. He allowed himself the pleasure of taking her hand. It was so soft he could imagine it caressing his body. *Whoa boy, take it easy here. You could be in over your head and not even know it.*

While they enjoyed the tasty rabbit stew and biscuits and later the juicy apple pie, André told her of his conversation with John Armstrong. She was a good listener and encouraged him with short comments, phrased carefully to use correct English. It was only when he reached the part about her leaving in August that she reverted back to her older speech patterns. "Ain't goin'." She folded her arms just under her bosom. André became too distracted watching the way that action pushed her breasts up so a small swell was visible at the top of her blouse.

"But I'm trying to help you. You originally ran away to go to Canada."

"Dat were den. Before I met you. Ain't goin'."

She leaned closer to him across the makeshift table. André couldn't help but notice a little more of her breasts became visible. He tried to avert his eyes so he could concentrate on the conversation. "Don't you see, here you run the risk of being captured and returned to your mistress?"

Again she replied, "Ain't goin'."

He tried again pointing out all the dangers here and the advantages in Canada. She was adamant. When she stood and whirled away from him and stormed out the front door, he noticed a faint scent. No doubt something Becky had produced from local wild roses. Probably he had smelled the same flowers a dozen times, but now it mingled with Renee's own scent and enchanted him.

André took a moment to compose his thoughts and followed Renee outside. She had walked around to the back of the cabin near the creek. She stood under the spreading branches of a large cottonwood tree, the moonlight drifting through the leaves playing a dappled symphony on her gleaming skin while the dress colors blended into shadow. He stopped and stared thinking he had never seen a more beautiful sight. A rustling in the underbrush caused Renee to spin back toward the cabin. Back into André who stood between her and the cabin. He felt her softness through his thin shirt. Suddenly her lips were pressed to his, and he knew he had lost the dispute. This time when she murmured, "Ain't goin'," he made no argument.

She led him back inside and sank onto the simple bed. She put her hand behind her back and with a few deft movements her dress fell away revealing pert breasts that smiled up at André. Although his mind said no, another part of his anatomy was responding in kind. She reached out a hand to guide him into the narrow bed. He lost that argument also.

 Chapter 17

July 5, 1856—Pottawatomie Creek, Kansas Territory

Becky helped Dan put away the supplies. When all was stored, Becky surprised him with a request. "The moon is full tonight. Wouldn't it be fun to take a dip in the creek before supper?"

Dan agreed at once. He had no idea what Becky planned on wearing–he assumed it would be less that the full-skirted high-necked blue frock she wore at the moment– but the idea of seeing her with less clothing and all wet was appealing. They walked back to the creek which flowed a few hundred yards behind their cabin. Mason and Dixon frolicked behind. Becky carried a blanket. Dan assumed it would be to drape over a tree branch so she would have some semblance of modesty while taking off the plain blue dress. She surprised him when she spread the blanket on the ground in a patch of grass near the creek's bank. He was even more stunned when she removed her dress revealing only white muslin bloomers and a chemise and turned to face him. "Aren't you going to take those dusty trousers and shirt off?" she asked.

Dan stared and gulped. "I um...Yes. I was just watching you. I mean…"

"Since we are married, I didn't think you would mind me bathing like this." She spread her hands and shrugged. The motion pressed two firm dark nipples against her tight chemise.

He hurriedly removed his outer garments and watched as Becky's eyes studied his broad chest. *Good thing she isn't looking any lower or she might be shocked.* He turned and quickly waded into the creek to his waist to hide the evidence of his arousal. "It's nice and warm. Come on in."

He heard her mumble something that sounded like "…going to get warmer."

"What did you say?" he asked.

"Just that warm is good." She stepped into the water, and as she approached, the wet muslin clung like a transparent skin.

Oh boy. She doesn't realize what she is doing to me.

Her next words took a decidedly interesting twist revealing Becky might know exactly what she was doing. "We've never talked about how many children you would like to have. Since I was an only child,

I would like a big family. How about you?"

Dan wasn't sure where this conversation might lead, but she had opened the door to a subject he needed to share with her: his and André's relationship. He began. "Speaking of only children, I haven't been exactly honest with you. There is something I need to tell you about André and me."

He stopped to consider how to best explain, but she just shrugged."He's your half-brother. I figured that out a long time ago."

"You knew? You aren't upset?"

"No, of course not. I like André. I know that happens in the South."

Dan took a step toward her. "It's not André I am ashamed of. It's my father. How he could do such a dishonorable thing."

"I figured that out too. While we are on this subject, you should know, Renee is pregnant," Becky confined.

"Oh, no!" Dan had not considered that possibility.

"Yes. About three months. We became a lot friendlier after you two left. We worked together on a dress for her and a few other things. She wanted me to tell you."

"Does André know? He's making arrangements for her to go to Canada on the Underground Railroad next month."

"She is going to tell him tomorrow."

"Why not tonight?" he asked.

"I think she plans on them being busy tonight."

Now Dan understood the separate supper arrangements.

Becky moved closer until her fully-visible nipples touched his chest. "Let's get back to deciding how many children we want, Husband."

His arms encircled her waist, and his lips moved inches above hers. "As you know, having children requires certain marital activities."

"That's why I brought the blanket down here." She pointed back to where the blanket, bathed in silvery moonlight, beckoned.

 Chapter 18

August 29, 1856—Pottawatomie Creek, Kansas Territory

Dan tossed the scraps to the pair of hogs rooting behind the cabin. He watched Becky tossing a handful of corn on the ground in front of the chicken coop door as she prepared to gather the eggs from the nests inside. Mason tugged at a bone Dixon's jaws had a firm grip on, and a play fight ensued between the two half-grown pups. He was pleased with the way things were going. He and André had jointly purchased these hogs. He had been able to obtain a fine cow and calf that the state of Missouri was giving to Southerners who were working their claim in Kansas. Just yesterday, they had harvested the last of the Doyle corn and stored it in the jointly owned barn they had built between the two cabins. The corn he and André had planted was going to be ready in about a week. André had offered to take the extra portion of this harvest into Topeka to sell to Mr. Jones at the general store. Dan offered to go along, but André stated he needed to stop and visit John Armstrong and Dan could take the excess of the next harvest. André hadn't said what his business with Armstrong was, but Dan assumed André wanted to tell him in person that Renee was now married to him and would not need the services of the Railroad.

André had amazed him. Upon finding out about Renee's pregnancy, he set out to the Shawnee Mission and found a preacher who agreed to marry the couple. Renee stayed out of sight as much as possible, but the softly rounded young matron bore little resemblance to the starved waif she had once been. It was doubtful any slave hunters would recognize her.

Dan spotted a familiar-looking rider approaching and quickly glanced toward André's cabin to be sure Renee was safely out of sight. Things had been going too well for them, but he knew it was only the calm before the storm. The territory was in an uproar. Fort Saunders and Fort Titus had been captured by Free-State men. Gov. Shannon was removed from office, and Acting Gov. David Woodson declared Kansas Territory in open rebellion. Dan had managed to remain neutral, but he had a premonition that the horseman fast approaching was about to change all that. He was going to be dragged back into the quagmire that was Kansas Territory today.

Sure enough the rider proved to be Rev. Martin White. White commented on how well Dan's leg had healed. "You don't look any the worse for wear. I trust that some of the care I took of you contributed to your recovery."

Dan didn't remind him that White had believed Dan almost dead when the good Reverend returned him to the cabin. He dared not tell him a runaway slave had effected the cure. He had no doubt that in spite of the friendship, White would have him sitting in jail in a few hours. White showed Dan his newest gun, a Walker Colt pistol. The weapon had a nine inch barrel and fired six .44 caliber balls with a single action hammer. White claimed it was deadly up to fifty yards and known to have struck a moving target at a hundred yards, a longer range than may rifles. After Dan had admired the gun, White cut to the heart of the matter. "I guess you've heard of the outrages those Free-Staters have been committing? Attacking our forts and killing our men, Fort Titus and Fort Saunders?"

Dan nodded. "I heard."

White chuckled. "Poor Col. Titus has left Kansas for the wilds of Florida. I guess he thinks the Seminoles and the alligators are less trouble than the Free-Staters. It's said that rascal Lane has assembled a vast army of Northerners and is marching them overland through Nebraska to attack us."

"Of course," Dan replied. "A person would have to be living in the outer reaches of Mongolia to have not heard that rumor."

"Well, it has gone far enough. We're going to strike back where it will hurt them the worst: Osawatomie, the home base of Old Brown."

Until this point, Dan had every intention of politely refusing to go. Brown was a different story. He had given Mahala Doyle his word he would try and avenge her husband and sons' deaths. "A strike at Osawatomie? Okay. I'm in for that. Come on up to the cabin. I need to explain to my wife. She is not going to be happy."

White replied, "The Bible says that a wife should be subject to her husband."

Becky greeted White coolly. She disliked the man for his slavery sentiments as well as for dragging Dan into a fight she felt he had no part in. Dan assured her he was honor-bound to go. Reminded her of what Brown had done to the Doyles and rode away on Chieftain, Little Thunder tucked into his scabbard, with Martin White to join up with the main body of militia. Within a few minutes in the saddle, both men were soaked with sweat from the unseasonably hot weather. The temperature had topped the one hundred mark with no relief in sight.

The conversation as the two men rode was desultory. Dan had become disillusioned with Martin White. He saw White as fanatical on the issue of slavery and felt they had little in common except that both men were Southerners. After White explained in loud angry terms how the "miserable abolitionists" had attacked his home and forced him to return to Missouri, they continued in silence. Dan considered the situation. No matter his feelings on slavery, he was still a Southerner. He strongly believed each state should have the right to govern itself. After all, hadn't the Revolutionary War been fought over just that issue? On a more practical side, his accent marked him as a Southerner in Kansas Territory. He knew there were just as many men on the Free-State side who were just as rabid in their view as White. In their eyes, his *views* meant nothing. His *accent*, everything. As soon as he opened his mouth they would attack him. Even had he not felt so strongly about states' rights, he was forced into the mold of Southerner here. His side was already chosen for him. Much as he would have preferred it, neutrality was not at question. Others who had protested neutrality had been shot and their claims ravaged by both sides. That and the fact that he was sworn to revenge the Doyles' killing kept him riding with White.

They met up with Captain John W. Reid and his party of four hundred mostly Missourians just before crossing the Marias des Cygnes, at Bundy's Ford, four miles northwest of Osawatomie. By now it was predawn, and Reid ordered White and a small group including Dan to scout out the area between them and Osawatomie. About a mile west of town, White raised his hand in a "stop" signal. With the others, Dan guided his horse off to the side of the road and looked in the direction White pointed. Two men on horseback were approaching.

The horseman in the lead, a stocky young man, greeted them. "Good morning, boys; are you going to Lawrence today?"

White studied him a moment before replying. "Why, I know you!" Accompanying the words, he raised his Walker Colt Pistol, fired at the man, shooting him dead in the road. His companion turned and tried to run his horse into the brush on the side of the road. White's large pistol barked again, stopping his retreat.

Dan protested angrily. "You just shot those men without giving them a chance to surrender. Hell, maybe they were not even part of Brown's group. That is murder."

White laughed. "Murder? I think not. I recognized those men." They are part of that pestiferous gang of Abolitionists." He pointed with his gun to the first body. "That is Fredrick Brown, Old Man Brown's son, and that other fellow is David Garrison, a close crony of Brown."

"Perhaps…," Dan began.

White interrupted. "They are the very horse thieves that pinched a herd of my cattle and several horses. If you check under the saddle of the sorrel Fred Brown was riding, you will find two small white patches shaped like a diamond. I also have my brand on the animal's rump."

Dan felt the blood pounding at his temples. He clenched his fists to keep from striking out at the preacher. "Still, you could have given them chance to surrender."

White shrugged. "This is war, boy. Since you are so outraged at me, ride back and tell Reid the alarm is no doubt given in the camp." To the man on his other side he barked, "Catch those horses and let's get going. We need to attack at once."

Glad to be out of White's presence, Dan rode back about half a mile where he met Reid's approaching troops and told the commander of the events. Reid did not seem unduly disturbed by Dan's report. "White just rid us of two of the damned Free-State boys." He raised his hand and signaled the two hundred plus men riding behind him the attack was on.

Dan wheeled his horse and fell in just behind Reid next to Jim Hale, whom he had met earlier. At least now they would be taking part in a more honorable form of battle.

They rode on to Osawatomie full tilt. Everything seemed a kaleidoscope of activity. Dan observed Brown's men, about forty or so, rush from a blockhouse to the timber on the south of the Marais des Cygnes, placing them between Reid's men and the river. The Free-Staters hunkered down behind tree trunks and for a few moments held their fire. It seemed they were waiting for their attackers to come closer. First one shot rang out, then a volley.

Dan ducked close to his horse's neck and fired in the general direction of Brown's men. All around him his comrades poured through the town toward the enemy. Dan turned Chieftain back along with the others in his line to allow them to fire while he reloaded. It became mechanical. Dan realized he was no longer afraid of being shot, just concentrated on firing at Brown's men hiding just past the timberline. It seemed to go on forever although he knew in actual time only a few minutes had passed. He considered the possibility one of his bullets might kill a man he did not even know. Perhaps one who had nothing to do with the Doyles' murders. He realized the thought did not worry him unduly. These men rode with Brown and upheld Brown's actions. That made them Dan's enemies.

Finally Hale, riding next to him as they reloaded, pointed and shouted over the gunfire, "We're bringing up the cannon. That will flush out those bastards."

Dan looked and saw the cannon being positioned. It barked only once before the Free-State men scrambled backward to the river. Dan made ready to pursue, but the command passed down the order to stop and reconnoiter the town. Dan, Hale, Frank Coleman, who had been a fellow prisoner after the Battle of Blackjack, and several other men were assigned to check the blockhouse where Brown had first attempted to mount a defense. Within, they found six men cowering behind the door. Coleman yanked one of the men up by his shirtfront. "You're the bastard that captured me at Blackjack. Charley Kaiser, right?"

The prisoner nodded. Coleman was for killing him on the spot, but Dan and Hale objected. "Let Captain Reid decide at a court marshal," Dan argued.

"Right, Frank. No question he will be found guilty and shot. You will have a clear conscience," Hale agreed.

"My conscience doesn't bother me at all when I step on a cockroach, either." Still muttering, Coleman released Kaiser to the others and allowed them to lead him to the wagon that was being used to contain prisoners. As they brought in their prisoners, one of the other group was triumphantly hustling a slight young man into the wagon. One of them announced, "We caught the best fish. This here is Spencer Brown, Old Brown's son."

Another man pointed to one of the prisoners Dan's group led out. "That'un's a traiter if'fin I ever saw one. A Missouri man turned Free-Stater." He spat on the ground and tried to grab the man, Billy Williams.

"Leave him be. He gets a fair trial tomorrow. Captain Reid decides his fate." Hale continued to push the prisoner into the wagon.

Dan noticed another group of militiamen setting fire to the houses they had already checked for stragglers. No women or children in the village meant they were expecting the attack. News seemed to travel on the winds here in Kansas Territory. What bothered Dan the worst was that John Brown had slipped away again. *Will I ever avenge my friends?*

The heat compounded by the rising flames of the village was almost unbearable. The men, now slowed by wagons of wounded comrades, prisoners and, of course, plunder, made their slow way back to camp on Bull Creek.

Reid planned to let his men rest a few days there. It was not to be. Dan and Hale, having rested a few hours Saturday night and spending most of Sunday drilling, decided to try and catch a few catfish for their supper. They wandered down the creek bank a few hundred yards. Suddenly, a horse and rider burst from the opposite bank. Dan dropped his fishing line and reached for his revolver. Hale did the same. "Halt," both men called almost in unison.

"Toss your weapons down and dismount." Dan leveled his revolver on a man dressed in a captain's militia uniform.

Hale took a cautious step to the side so he and Dan were separated enough to make it difficult for the rider to attempt a shot at one man without the other being able to retaliate, and said, "If you even twitch funny I'll plug you."

The horseman sneered but complied and tossed his revolver and rifle on the bank. Although he now had no weapon at easy reach, he appeared confident. "I would drop those little guns and try to run back to your pigsty of a camp before my men arrive to dispose of you like pesky mosquitoes. Tell them Captain Joe Cook is here to avenge what you swine did at Osawatomie."

He studied Dan's face carefully. "Aha. You I will make a special point of shooting in the gut just to watch you bleed to death."

Dan returned the stare without flinching. Recognition slowly dawned. He understood the murderous rage he had witnessed in Frank Coleman yesterday. He would enjoy shooting this man himself and have no qualms. He raised his revolver, but before he could fire, he heard the sound of many hooves approaching rapidly. The horseman used the slight distraction to spur his horse and gallop into the trees from which he had emerged. The setting sun blinded the Southerners as the horseman galloped to join his fast-approaching cavalry.

Dan motioned for Hale to follow him as he sprinted toward camp. "What's up? What's so bad about a few Free-State boys? We can whip them just like we did Brown," panted Hale.

"Maybe," Dan answered, "but don't you wonder why that man was so confident when we had the drop on him?"

Hale replied, "Didn't give it much thought."

Dan shook his head as he continued toward Reid's tent. "Remember all that talk about Lane's giant Army of the North?"

Puzzled, Hale replied, "Yeah, so?

Dan turned to face him as they reached Reid's tent. "'Captain Joe Cook' is really Captain James H. Lane. He is leading in an army that vastly outnumbers us. Now do you understand why we need to disband?"

 Chapter 19

September 1, 1856—Pottawatomie Creek, Kansas Territory

André approached the cave from the north side. He used a different route each time he came here. There could be no clear trail leading to the cave. In the clearing just above the cave's mouth, he stopped and whistled an old slave tune. It was *Wade in the Water*. He recalled slaves back home in Louisiana singing this very song. Even as a child he knew it had some special meaning, but because he spent most of his life with Dan and the other house servant, he was never quite sure about that meaning. He understood it now. On the last chorus and verse, he stopped whistling and actually sang. His voice was a clear tenor that carried well.

Wade in the Water, wade in the water, children.
Wade in the Water. God's gonna trouble the water.

Who are those children all dressed in Blue?
God's gonna trouble the water.
Must be the ones that made it through.
God's gonna trouble the water.

As he neared the end of the verse, he heard a slight rustle, and the first of the runaway slaves, a tall very dark man, appeared at the edge of the clearing. Several more emerged until the clearing was filled with people, old and young, men and women.

"Ya'll done good. Hardly made a sound. Keep doin' lik' that, and we gonna get you to the promised land." André's cheerful encouragement belied his inner thoughts. *Lord, how in the hell am I going to get fourteen people through strange woods at night all the way to Prairie City?* "Jus' a few things afore we start. We gonna stay off the main road twixt it and the creek. We head almost due north until we reach Bull Creek, then we swing west a bit. All the way, we stay near the water. Ya'll know why?" All the heads nodded. "If we hear any dogs, it could mean slave hunters. Like the song says, wade in the water. Dogs can't get your scent if you are in water. One more thing, do not make a sound. Walk quietly watching where you put yore feet. The sound of a branch snappin' carries a long way in the woods. Naturally no talkin' or singin'. If you should get lost, I guess if you got this far, you know to use that star for a marker." He pointed to the North Star. "Are you all ready?" All the heads nodded more vigorously this time.

All was quiet until they reached the Marais des Cygnes. Wading into small creeks was one thing. This river was wider and deeper. The people drew near André. "Sir, mos' of us cain't swim. We's gonna drown if'n we go into that." Fear showed in many eyes.

"No, you won't drown. We will all hold hands. I will go first. I can swim. Anybody else can swim?" André saw two men nod. "Okay. I got a rope in my pack. We tie it around everyone's waist. Then those of us who swim go across first and the rest just do like we do and let the rope pull you across. It may not even be over your head as this river floods and the depths change all the time."

With a bit of splashing and a few tears the group crossed the river. The trek proceeded at a good pace with no more incidents except flushing out a few nocturnal animals until they approached Bull Creek. Here André stopped and listened. He could hear sounds of a large encampment. A few flickering fires warned them away. With a gesture and just a few whispered directions, André led the party west away from the camp. Even though it was now near the middle of the night, the camp seemed awake and bustling. André took no chances. He had no idea if there was a trail leading parallel, but he was not bringing his first group of runaways anywhere near that camp.

He led them due west following twisted trails through the forest probably made by deer as they came to the creek to drink. Much of the time they needed to stoop to avoid having their faces cut by crisscrossing vines. Shortly they crossed a large road. André assumed this was the road to Lawrence, so after crossing cautiously, they paralleled the road traveling mostly northwest until they came to a deeply rutted road running east and west. André breathed a sigh of relief. He remembered the detailed geography lesson he had gotten from John Armstrong. *It's the South Route to Pikes Peak Road. Follow it west, and it leads me right to the road to the Reverend Wiley Jones's claim.*

His confidence restored, André considered the options. It was still far from dawn and the road would provide easier walking thus making quicker time. He weighed the possibilities and decided to lead them directly along the road instead of the more prudent parallel trails that may or may not have existed. The plan worked well until they rounded a bend in the road. Suddenly they were face to face with a large bearded man who was relieving himself by the side of the road. The man eyed them suspiciously. "Well what have we here? A big parcel of runaway niggers. Looks like I earn a nice purse tonight." He pulled an old flintlock pistol from his belt and pointed it directly at André.

The slave hunter seemed to realize as long as he controlled André, the obvious conductor, the others would be too frightened to act. For the most part he was right. Most of the slaves, the women and older men, huddled together. Total fear and defeat showed on their faces. Only the tall man, André recalled his name was Henry, who had been the first one to answer André's signal stood apart as if ready to fight.

The only move that occurred to André was to cause the slave hunter to look away for a moment. He tried to signal Henry to move farther out of the man's range of vision. Henry seemed to pick up the clue and stepped closer to the woods at the side of the road. He appeared to stumble, drawing the slave hunter's gaze for a second. It was enough. André lunged forward, hitting the big slave hunter hard on his right side. At the same time, he yanked the Bowie knife he had secreted in his boot. He realized he had no choice but to the kill the man.

The gun hit the ground and fired the primed shot. André had gone down with the big man and now had his right arm pinned under the man's shoulder. The slave hunter was trying to get a grip on André's arm, but with a sudden burst of strength he didn't know he possessed, André jerked his arm free and in one quick motion slashed backwards against the man's throat. Blood spurted skyward. The warm liquid flowed over André's still outstretched arm. He had no idea killing was so easy. Or so hard. He felt the overwhelming need to vomit. He staggered to his feet and reached into the pitted ruts of the road. His mother had taught him the commandments since he was a tiny boy. He remembered her saying, "'Thou shall not kill.' Chile, dat's a big'un. The Lord don't forgive that'un easy."

André knew it was only a matter of time before people from the camp they had passed would hear the shot and be here to investigate. There might even be a fellow slave hunter nearby. They often traveled in pairs, splitting the bounties.

He felt no guilt and wondered at his lack of it for a moment. *If I had not killed that man, he would have killed me and returned all these people to slavery or death. I did what I needed to do. He had a description of me and would end my usefulness to the Underground Railroad and most likely my life as well.*

Henry and a few of the other men in the group had pulled the dead body off the road so it would not be found so easily. He approached André. "Yo okay, Mr. André."

"Yes. I am fine." As he said the words, he realized they were true. Her felt no guilt, only a pressing need to get these people to safety. "Let's go. We need to get to the safe house before dawn." He splashed a bit of water on his hands and wiped them with his bandana, and they walked briskly down the road.

They covered the last few miles without incident. When they reached the circuit rider's cabin, a lantern hung from his hitching post indicating it was safe to bring the slaves in. André knocked with the special knock he had been told to use, and the door was opened instantly by a small, blue-eyed woman. She seemed to be in her fifties but was wiry and vigorous. "I'm Abigail. Reverend Wiley is down in the cellar preparing a safe place. There is food and water. Welcome." Her gaze took in all the slaves, and they accepted her invitation to proceed to the cellar at once.

Do you want to stay the night?" Abigail asked André.

Too weary to speak much, he just shook his head. "No thank you, Ma'am."

"Let me get you a bite to eat and a fresh canteen of water for your return trip." She hurried into the kitchen.

The reverend came up from the cellar and pulled the trap door shut. He placed a rag rug over it, and the floor appeared one continuous span. "You did the Lord's work, young man," he addressed André.

"I had to kill a slave hunter who stopped us," André said.

The old man did not change expressions. "As I said, you did the Lord's work."

It was well past dawn when André reached Bull Creek. On this return trip he continued to skirt the main road and follow the side trails. Normally he would not have hesitated to use the road. Although there were some unscrupulous slave hunters who might try to destroy his papers and re-enslave him, it was a small risk. This morning he was being cautious because of the large gathering of men near Bull Creek and the fact that he did not want to be identified anywhere nearby when the body of a dead slave hunter turned up. He reached the Marais des Cygnes River before he decided to stop and eat the cornbread and ham the Joneses had given him. He was tired, dirty and still felt like he bore traces of the dead man's blood on his body in spite of the fact that he had washed carefully before he left the Joneses.

The river was cool and refreshing. André enjoyed one last dip before he stepped ashore and began pulling his clothes back on. He had one leg into his trousers when something cold and hard pressed into his back. "Get your hands in the air and turn around slowly," the rough voice intoned.

Oh Lord. They found the body and know I did it. I'm a goner now.
André let go of the waistband of his trousers and turned as the voice

commanded. "I ain't done nothin'...," he began then started laughing.

Standing behind him stood Dan. Dan lowered the gun and joined in the laughter. "André, you're the last person I expected to find out here."

André finished getting dressed, and the two men started home. Dan persisted. "What are you doing out here swimming this hour of the morning anyway."

André hated lying to Dan, but the less Dan knew, the less trouble he could be in if André was caught. "Just wanted to get away for a bit." *Besides this seemed a good place to wash off the reminders of the man I killed last night.* To deflect any further questions André asked, "How come you're so jumpy and quick with that gun anyway?"

"Remember that man who wanted to hang me back in Lawrence? Colonel James Lane?"

"Sure, aside from your close call with him the whole territory knows of Jim Lane."

"Well, I almost shot him last night. He led his Army of the North against us up at Bull Creek where we were camping. Incidentally, when we raided Osawatomie, Brown escaped again. I think that man has more lives than a cat."

André remembered his first sight of Drury Doyle. The Doyles had treated him fairly. Then he remembered the fiery-eyed man who led Doc and his friends to freedom. He was not sure if he was sorry or glad the man escaped. "Too bad." *Oh what a tangled web we weave when first we practice to deceive.* Sir Walter Scott's analysis in *Marmion* still held true, André thought.

Dan continued, not noticing the hesitation in André's voice. "You know, I may have killed men in that fight, but somehow it doesn't bother me. Can you understand that?"

Only too well, my brother. "This is turning into war. In war, men kill for what they believe in." *As I had to do last night.*

André placed an arm on Dan's shoulder. "We are family. Remember that. Let's hope war never pushes us onto opposite sides."

"True, I'm a Southerner, but I don't want to go to war just because someone is from the North. I don't want them trying to run things their way, but I don't want to go to war over it. Seems like we should be able to work things out peacefully."

"I hope so," André replied. *What about slavery? Will that workout peacefully?*

As if reading his mind, Dan commented, "That fellow I met in Topeka, Jo Shelby from Missouri, seems his cousin, Frank Blair, is going to run for Congress on a plan to provide compensation for slave owners to free slaves and resettle them in their own country. He is friends with some lawyer in Illinois named Lincoln that agrees with that idea. Maybe people like that with lots of money can show us all a peaceful way out of this mess."

"Maybe, but I doubt it," André replied skeptically.

"Well, Brown paying for what he did to the Doyles is one thing. War is another. I will remain neutral," Dan declared.

"That newspaper in Atchison, the *Squatter Sovereign*, had an article recently about that. I don't remember the whole article, but I do remember the last sentence of it," André said.

"Oh yeah," Dan asked. "What did that say?"

André quoted the article. "'If civil war is to be the result in such a conflict, there cannot be, and will not be, any neutrals recognized.'"

 Chapter 20

September 9, 1856—Pottawatomie Creek, Kansas Territory

Dan and André were both soaked with sweat and streaked with dust. The sun was blazing overhead, but the two men were as happy as if they were enjoying a balmy day sitting in the shade enjoying a cool drink. They had just harvested the last of the crop they had so hurriedly planted when they first arrived in May.

Becky and Renee had been laboring almost as hard. The women had been dealing with all the other chores: milking the cow, slopping the pigs, feeding the chickens and the myriad of other small tasks that occupied a Kansas farmer from dawn to dusk. In addition, the wild plums that grew in the nearby thickets had ripened and needed to be picked. Both women were covered with scratches but had picked bushels of the juicy fruit and were canning at the same time they were preparing meals and cold drinks to serve the men when they took brief breaks from the corn harvest.

They were not in the mood for company when André spotted the lone rider approaching the front of Dan's cabin.

André spoke first. "I'll swing around behind your cabin and make sure Renee stays out of sight."

"Good idea," Dan replied. "I don't recognize the man, so he could be up to no good."

He sauntered around the house and greeted the stranger. "Howdy. What can I do for you?"

He noticed Becky behind the front window and was willing to bet she had his rifle in her hands. The man dismounted and looked around. "Nice place you have here."

"We think so," Dan replied noncommittally.

"Are you Daniel Fitzpatrick?"

"I am."

"It appears there may be a problem with this claim. I'm James Hogan, representing Sheriff Samuel Jones." He handed Dan an official looking piece of paper. "This states you either have to prove ownership of this claim or vacate no later than thirty days from today."

"I have a perfectly good deed for this claim signed over to me by the former owner. Do you want to see it?"

The man had already remounted. He shook his head. "No. I'm just the process server. If you have something that supports your claim you need to present it to the proper authorities in Lecompton at Constitution Hall. Land Office is on the first floor."

Dan looked more closely at the paper he held as he entered the cabin. It looked official and was signed by the territory land office official. The paper stated that another person had contested his claim and named Dan as an adverse claimant. It gave a date when the matter would be heard and where Dan could present any proof of his rights to the claim. The man's name, William Baldridge, meant nothing to Dan, but the two witnesses set off an immediate alarm. He let out a low whistle. "Look at this."

He showed the paper to Becky and André. Renee, unable to read, stood awkwardly to one side. Dan pointed to the witnesses' signatures. Becky picked up on it first. "Henry Laine and Joseph Cook? Too much coincidence for me. Even the claimant's name. Jim Lane's wife's maiden name is Baldridge. Somehow when he saw you last week, he knew you had not fled the territory. He decided to track us down and get back at us for embarrassing him when you escaped."

"I doubt Lane's father-in-law, the former governor of Indiana, wants this claim. It's just Lane's way of making problems for us," Dan said.

Becky shuddered. "I'll never forget the sound of his voice as he yelled, 'I'll make you pay a thousand times.' I have an awful feeling this is just the beginning."

She sank into a nearby chair. Renee began to rub her back gently.

"What can he do beyond being a nuisance?" Dan stepped over and took her hand. "I'll leave for Lecompton first thing tomorrow. I'll take care of it. Don't worry, darling."

"Renee and I will stay here and be sure he doesn't try any sneak attack while you are away," André said.

Renee nodded. "André has been teaching me to use a rifle so I can help too. Becky, you can give me some more lessons in reading while Dan is gone. I'll show you a new recipe. We will never let anyone hurt you."

The two men spent a good part of the night loading the corn and covering it with hay to keep it fresh. After just a few hours' troubled sleep, Dan was seated on the wagon at daybreak headed for Lecompton. He and André had decided since he had to go that far, he would take the excess corn into Topeka or even find a store in Lecompton that would buy it. He was not too worried about the phony claim affidavit. If need be, he had the two hundred dollars to purchase it from the Land Office. It did worry him that Lane would take the time while riding around terrorizing the people of the Law and Order Party to investigate and locate his whereabouts. Dan had no doubt Lane knew that Dan and Becky were married. Remembering the look Lane had given him at Bull Creek, Dan suspected that while Lane was just toying with him now, the man's revenge could continue as something much more dangerous. He had complete faith in André's ability to take care of things on the home front, but he was concerned. He sensed an incipient madness in Lane, making him capable of dangerous acts.

Dan spent little time in camp that night and arrived in Lecompton near daybreak. The land office was not open yet, but he saw a general store and entered. The owner, James G. Bailey, quickly agreed to purchase the corn and paid a fair price.

Now to take care of James Lane's nonsense. Dan entered the land office and found the entire office in an uproar. He approached the counter with the summons and Mrs. Doyle's deed in his hand..

"Can I he'p ya?'" The speaker was an older man with a full beard.

"I certainly hope so," Dan replied.

He explained the situation and informed the man of his suspicions that this was personal, not a question about the legitimacy of his claim.

"Based on those two names, it sure does look like you are right about that devil Lane up to another kind of his devilment." The man peered at the witness signatures as if he would love to get his hands on the signers. "Still, the law is the law and I have to treat this as if it is a legitimate action. It is possible that this is just a coincidence and there really are three people by these names. We'll place your deed in evidence and notify you if this so-called claimant appears on the hearing date. If he doesn't show and prove a prior claim, you can pay the claim costs, $1.25 per acre, and the claim is legally yours. The Doyles had not proven up on the claim, that is, held and improved it for five years, so you need to pay the fee to place a preemptive claim."

"Thank you so much." Dan turned to leave, but the man called him back.

"In case you might have a hankering to confront Colonel Lane or Colonel Jo Cook or whatever he is calling hisself today, I heard tell some of our boys that are sound on the goose are holed up at Hickory Point waiting for that particular Yankee devil to attack them."

The idea of confronting Lane was irresistible. Having a gun in his hand and the opportunity to use it on the man was even more so. "What are you talking about?"

The clerk explained, "A bunch of Kickapoo Rangers, 'bout fifty men led by Nathaniel Boydston, are in those few log buildings at Hickory Point. Lane and his Second Kansas State Militia and Col. James A. Harvey are massing on our boys there. Our new governor, Geary, has arrived in the territory and ordered Lane and his men to disband, but since when have they ever paid any mind to orders they don't like?"

"Any idea how many?" Dan asked.

"Some say the Free-Staters have fifteen hundred men. If you are a Law and Order man, we need you badly up there. A group of our younger men is assembling behind Bailey's General Store if you would be inclined to ride with them."

"Maybe I'll get in a lucky shot and end the bastard's harassment that way."

The clerk answered, "I'll be pulling for you."

Dan rushed back to the general store and arranged for the wagon to remain in the store owner's care. He used one of the dray horses, Toby. It seemed ironic to use for the fight ahead the bay he and Becky had liberated from Lane in Lawrence. He wished he had Chieftain but had to make do with the sway-backed bay. At least he had a mount. He saw many of the men heading toward Hickory Point on foot. Dan found himself riding next to a young man named Lon. Dan told Lon about the events at Osawatomie and Bull Creek.

In turn, Lon relayed what had been happening in this area for the past few days. "A bunch of our boys roared into Osawkie on the eighth and got a bit high-spirited. Naturally, they got back at us. A bunch of them hit Indianola, stole some guns and horses, and dumped all the whiskey into the street. They rode off with most of the valuables in town."

Dan replied, "That is happening all over the territory. It's reached the point where no one is safe. Maybe we just all need to get along."

Lon looked at Dan if he had just spoken treason. "Are you really going to let these people do whatever they want to us and get away with it?"

Dan thought about Lane's attempt first to hang him in Lawrence and now to run him off his claim. "You're right. I'm not going to let Lane and his bullies get away with anything."

Lon nodded, his faith in Dan as a fellow Southerner apparently confirmed. "Even worse, just yesterday, Lane attacked and captured a bunch of North Carolina boys on Slough Creek."

When they arrived at Hickory Point, they circled around into the settlement. Dan saw a large double log house on the north side of the Atchison-Topeka stage road. He had been told a Capt. H. A. Lowe lived in that house. There were several buildings near the bottom of a hill and just west of a small stream of water. A few stunted trees and bushes flanked the stream banks south of the road with a cluster of trees to the north of the house. A log blacksmith's shop and a few sheds and outbuildings were west of the house and on somewhat higher ground. A portion of the hill partly hid the buildings from the Free-State troops located at the top of the hill.

Dan, along with the other new arrivals, sought out Captain Lowe stationed in the blacksmith shop, and reported to him. Just as they approached the captain, a horseman rode in from the Free-State camp carrying a white handkerchief tied to a ramrod. He galloped down the hill waving his flag as he went. Lowe and his two lieutenants stepped out to meet the rider. The conference was very brief. Lowe accepted a paper the rider handed to him. He read it quickly and abruptly handed it back. Dan heard him say to rider, "Take this dirty paper back to Colonel Harvey and tell him we will fight him and all the hireling cutthroats and assassins he can bring against us."

Lowe returned to the cover of the blacksmith shop. His face was red with fury. He informed all of the men within earshot, "Lane demanded unconditional surrender but didn't have the guts to even sign the paper. He had Harvey sign it."

General Lane formed his cavalry to the south of the road. From a window inside the blacksmith shop, Dan could see them when they crossed the stream and occupied an elevation about four hundred yards southeast of the shop where Dan and the other Law and Order men crouched with their rifles at the ready. Some of the chinking had been knocked from between the logs to give them more places to fire on the enemy. Dan looked for a clean shot at Lane; he would have taken it even thought the order had been to "hold fire"; however, Lane was careful to always remain where others in the troop shielded him from any such stray shots.

A movement caught Dan's eye. It was one of the men on foot arriving from Lecompton. Instead of trying to sneak in from the side, he dashed directly in front of Lane's troops. The man was young, around fifteen or sixteen, and carried a condemned U.S. Army rifle across his shoulder.

One of Lane's cavalrymen galloped toward the new arrival. The boy saw his pursuer and changed course, veering a little to the north. He ran swiftly toward the trees and bushes on the creek. He had a head start on the horseman, but it would be touch and go. The horseman was within one hundred yards of the runner when he reined up his horse, quickly dismounted and took deliberate aim at the boy. Seeing his pursuer about to fire, the boy stooped as he ran and loped into the safety of the blacksmith shop almost on all fours. The bullet whistled harmlessly into the log frame, and the boy sank to the ground gasping for air.

The cavalryman inserted a fresh cartridge in his breech-loader, swung himself back into the saddle, and rode rapidly in the direction of the shop. When he reached directly in front of it and was in full view of all of us, he suddenly checked his horse, took a rapid aim and fired. The bullet whizzed by and entered through the window nearest Dan. Dan was too intent on watching the drama to return fire. Apparently the rest of the troops were too surprised to act either. The horseman wheeled around, spurred his horse, and galloped away. A few scattering shots rang out from the buildings. The rider swayed in his saddle from side to side, while his horse galloped zigzag back and forth across the road toward his comrades.

"We got him! He's shot!" someone cried out.

As the swaying horseman neared his line, he suddenly straightened and threw his hand into the air in a rude gesture, then galloped, clearly unhurt, back into the shelter of the bushes to join his fellow Free-Staters.

Dan joined in congratulating the new arrival, a young fellow named Johnny. "Boy, that was a close one. I'm so glad you made it alive." He wasn't sure if he was glad or sorry the reckless Free-Stater had also escaped unscathed.

Then Dan was drawn back to his post by a shout. "Their cavalry is approaching. Prepare to fire."

When Dan returned to his window post, he saw that the cavalry had indeed closed some of the distance. Dan focused on the leader, probably a captain; his coat was thrown aside and his vest was open in front revealing a single suspender. It looked like he was intending on leading an assault on the log buildings. Not a smart move. The horseman stopped at about fifty feet and began firing. Dan returned fire. He noticed many of the enemy shots were falling short and ending harmlessly in the dust several feet in front of the shop. The ones that were covering the distance pinged into the thick logs shielding the occupants of the building. The only danger was if anyone exposed themselves in a window or doorway at the wrong moment.

"Save your ammunition, boys, unless you are using a Sharp's Rifle and have a clear shot at one of them bastards," Lowe shouted. "They can't touch us."

Dan knew there was another group of cavalry firing on them from the other side of the river, but those men were so far out of range they were even less threat.

From somewhere in the far corner of the shop, one man, a grizzled mountaineer from the Appalachian area, let out a high-pitched cry. It sounded like the call of a male wolf in heat. Some of the other fighters picked up the call, and soon the air reverberated with the banshee howl that could send shivers down brave opponents' spines.

The terrifying yells sent up by the defiant rebels in the blacksmith shop either had succeeded in demoralizing the enemy, or Lane and Harvey must have realized they would never dislodge the Southerners without heavy artillery. Lane soon called a retreat.

Lowe walked around the building clapping men on the shoulder and thanking them for their efforts. The North Carolina men wanted to leave the settlement, but Lowe requested they all remain another day. "I know those bastards will try again tomorrow. They will bring in that damned cannon, Sacramento, that they stole from Franklyn. That's what they did that when they attacked Fort Titus."

The men all agreed to stay and defend Hickory Point one more day. Dan was uneasy about leaving Becky alone but realized he could not abandon his comrades. Then, too, Lane was his biggest worry, and while the man was here attacking Hickory Point he could not be harassing Dan's family.

Much of the conversation around the campfire that night centered on the brash cavalryman who had almost ridden into their camp to shoot at the late arrival. "Johnny, my boy, you're a lucky son of a gun," one grizzled soldier informed him.

"Don' ah know it," the boy replied.

The old-timer continued. "Know who that was a chasing ya?"

"Yeah. A damned Free-Stater who cain't shoot straight," Johnny replied.

"Oh, he's supposed ta be a good shot. I'd knowed him befor'. The fellow's name is James Butler Hickok.

"Well," Johnny replied, "he shore was shootin' a lil' wild today an' ain't I glad he were."

One old timer commented, "Actin' like that, he sure won't live ta comb his hair gray lessen he calms down a mite."

The next day dawned with not a cloud in the sky. Sure enough, when Dan stepped cautiously out of the shop to look around, he saw signs of Harvey's men approaching. He spotted the captured cannon from Franklin nicknamed Sacramento. He quickly ran back into the shop and alerted the others. Within minutes, a huge explosion shook the roof of the shop. One of Sacramento's cannonballs had pierced the roof just above them. One soldier jumped out of harm's way. When the smoke cleared, the soldier looked toward the man who had been on his right. "Oh God, they got Charlie Newhall."

Several men rushed to see if they could offer aid, but it was too late. Charlie was dead. The first to reach the victim's side shook his head. "That there ball musta landed right atop of him. Ain't nothing no un couldh'd done."

No one else was seriously injured, but spirits were sobered by this, their first casualty.

Harvey continued firing the cannon and had his men fire muskets, but now the defenders dropped to the floor at the first sign of a flash from the cannon and used the windows only to fire and immediately duck back.

Peering out the window, Dan saw no sign of Lane's troops. Harvey, unsupported, had no choice but to withdraw eventually. The two sides struck an uneasy truce.

Dan and the rest of the Pro-Slavery men remained encamped again that night to be sure it was not a trick. Perhaps as soon as the reinforcements rode away, Lane and Harvey might swoop down and destroy helpless Hickory Point.

However, around midday, a scout dispatched by Colonel P. St. George Cooke arrived in their midst. He asked who was in command and reported to Captain Lowe. "Sir, I am here to inform you to disband your men. The troops who were unlawfully assembled and attacked you yesterday and the day before have been captured and are on their way to Fort Leavenworth at this moment."

Everyone tossed their hats in the air and fell to clapping one another on the back. The scout advised them to return to our homes as Governor Geary had ordered all militia disbanded until he re-formed a new Kansas Militia. He said the governor realized they were besieged so were not in violation.

Dan had to ask. "Sir," he addressed the scout, "can you tell us how many men you captured and under whose command?"

"It's no secret," the scout replied. "There were a hundred and one men under the command of Colonel Harvey."

Someone else asked what Dan most wanted to know. "What about Colonel Lane?"

The scout couldn't hide his contempt. "Colonel Lane decided to honor Governor Geary's order and withdrew his men back to Topeka on the thirteenth without informing Colonel Harvey. The militia was disbanded temporarily, and no one knows where Lane has gone to ground."

 Chapter 21

September 17, 1856—Pottawatomie Creek, Kansas Territory

Dan breathed a sigh of relief when he started up the road to his cabin. Everything looked peaceful. Becky and Renee were on the porch setting some plums on a rack in the sun to dry. He didn't see André but felt sure the women would not be going about ordinary business if there was any problem.

As he pulled the wagon to the porch, Becky ran down to embrace him and Renee waved. André came out from the barn covered with hay and carrying a pitchfork. Dan waved to his brother and Renee and enfolded Becky in his arms. He suddenly realized how much he had come to love this woman fate had tossed in his path. "I'm so glad you are safe," Becky murmured.

André waved back and called out, "You missed all the excitement."

"What happened?" Dan clutched Becky tighter.

André replied, "Wasn't really a big deal. Someone snuck up on the cabin and tried to toss a torch on the roof. Luckily we were all awake and talking inside and heard it hit the roof. I ran out with my gun, but by the time I got out the door, whoever tossed it was galloping away. I would never have caught him, and besides I didn't want to leave the women alone in case it was a trick."

Becky took up the tale. "We all sat up most of the night, but nothing else happened so maybe it was just some crazy guy who liked to set fires."

André shrugged. "We heard Lane was up at Hickory Point, so it could have hardly been him."

Dan replied, "It could have been Lane."

He explained the events of the past few days and Lane's abandonment of his fellow Free-Staters. "We'll just have to be extra vigilant. Sooner or later Lane will have something more important on his mind than harassing us." He tried to believe what he said.

The rest of 1856 passed more peacefully. True to his word, Governor

Geary had disbanded all militia. He used the Federal troops to try and maintain order and for the most part succeeded, but unrest was growing. Now instead of bullets, ballots were the weapons of choice in Kansas Territory. The bullets still flew but not as often and not between large militia groups.

Geary had originally been welcomed by the Law and Order party but soon swung toward the Free-State Party. Like the previous governors, Geary could not quell the two opposing forces in the territory. Reeder had lasted thirteen months and Shannon eleven months. After serving less than six months, Geary tendered his resignation and armed with two guns, left the territory during the night and returned to Washington on March 21. He said he feared for his life and began a series of public speaking tours around the country on the lawlessness in Kansas Territory.

For Dan and André and their wives, life was a quiet routine. Farm animals needed to be cared for, crops needed planting and life took on a natural rhythm.

On the night of December 20, André came running to Dan's cabin. "Becky! Becky!" he shouted. "It's time. Come quick."

Instantly alert, Becky and Dan hurried over to André's cabin. Inside, Renee lay on the bed moaning. André paced back and forth across the small room stopping to clutch her hand and murmur, "It's going to be fine."

Becky took charge instantly. "Dan, take André and get a big kettle of water boiling." Directing her attention to Renee, she murmured, "It really is going to be fine. Let me help you raise that shift. And remember to try and breathe like we talked about."

Renee nodded. Her face was covered with sweat, and her eyes revealed her fear. "I can feel it coming. My water broke, and I think it's going to be soon."

Becky stroked her friend's damp forehead. "Good. I'll be here and help as it comes."

"Thank…Ohh ohh." A scream finished off her words.

Outside the closed door of the small second room André had added shortly after he and Renee married, Dan struggled to get the embers in the fireplace to flare up under a large kettle of water. "I never had this much trouble getting a fire blazing before."

A scream escaped the closed door, and André moaned. "Man, she's so young. Women die in childbirth all the time. Suppose…"

Dan interrupted. "Don't even think that. She will be fine. Becky has read everything she could find about midwifeing."

"Reading and doing is two different things," André insisted.

To the two waiting men, it seemed like days, but in reality it was just as dawn was breaking when Becky emerged holding a squirming bundle. She held it out to André. "It's a girl."

André reached for the bundle with shaking hands. "My daughter."

No one contradicted him.

André held the baby reverently. "Can I see Renee?"

"She may be sleeping," Becky cautioned.

But when André stopped in front of the bed with the precious bundle, Renee's eyes were wide open. "Isn't she beautiful?"

André agreed. "She is that. Just like her mama. I think she has your eyes. What do you want to name her?"

"I want you to name her," Renee said.

"Me?" André asked.

"Yes. If it wasn't for you, she might not even be alive. I want her to be part of you too."

"She is the same as my daughter. I want to call her Dawn. Dawn because she came at dawn and I brought you up from the cave at dawn. Dawn Rebecca because Becky has helped us both so much."

"Dawn." Renee tested the name. "I like that. Also, it's the dawn of a new time. This child was born in freedom. And Becky has been my first white friend." Renee's eyes were drifting closed when André settled the baby in the crook of her arm and left them both to sleep.

 Chapter 22

May 1858—Pottawatomie Creek, Kansas Territory

Dan surveyed the new field of wheat stretching between his and André's cabins near the barn. It was almost ready for harvest. André and he had considered long and hard before deciding to use some of the fields for wheat instead of the corn they had grown at first. It was a good decision. The weather had worked with them, and they should have a really good harvest. In spite of their prosperous looking future, Dan had felt a sense of unease deepening since the Marais du Cygnes massacre. He replayed what he knew of the event in his mind.

John Brown and his crony, James Montgomery, calling themselves Jayhawkers, had been harassing the Missouri border counties with slave stealing raids. Dan had mixed feelings with the raiders taking the slaves to freedom. He felt slaves should be free through a legal process, not by being stolen from their owners. If the raiders had paid the owners, that would have been different. Instead they just stole not only the slaves but anything else not nailed down, then burned the homes and barns.

The Missourians had banded together under a Col. Charles Hamilton. Hamilton had come from Georgia to the territory and settled in a place called Trading Post but was forcibly driven out by a band of Free-Staters who had raided the place, dumped all the whiskey in the street and informed Hamilton and his friends that they had better hightail it back to Missouri.

They did but shortly after Hamilton sent an open letter to the Free-State residents remaining in Trading Post. It urged any Pro-Slavery men "to come out of the territory at once, as we are coming up there to kill snakes, and will treat all we find there as snakes."

Hamilton wasn't making an idle threat. On May 19, 1858, thirty men under Hamilton's leadership crossed into Kansas and headed for Trading Post.

They took prisoner eleven Free-State men, none of which were armed. In fact most were former neighbors of Hamilton and did not believe he would do them serious harm. Hamilton led the way into a defile surrounded by the mounds that characterize the area. There his men herded the Free-State men into a line, and Hamilton's men formed another line on the side of the ravine. Hamilton gave the order to fire, sending off the first shot himself. The victims fell. Then Hamilton dismounted his firing squad to finish the job with pistols. In their blood lust, five of the Free-State men were killed, five wounded, and one feigned death and escaped unharmed. Hamilton's men must have believed the wounds fatal and neglected to finish their bloody work.

Even most Pro-Slave men felt this went too far. Newspapers across the nation denounced the massacre as an outrage. Governor Denver –he had replaced Governor Walker, Geary's replacement who had lasted less than five months– seemed confused and first issued a warrant for Montgomery's arrest. The Lecompton Constitution, like the earlier Leavenworth constitution and Topeka Constitution, had been rejected by the United States Congress. Kansas Territory, as usual, was in a state of confusion.

An event that worried Dan almost as much as the massacre had occurred the following day and was almost as controversial. James Lane had shot and killed a neighbor in a claim dispute. The story circulating was that Lane and another Free-State man, Giaus Jenkins, both laid claim to a certain piece of land. Lane had earlier sold a portion of the land to Jenkins, but Jenkins had fallen behind in his payments and Lane took the land back. Jenkins continued to claim the land where he had built a small cabin. The well was on the portion containing the cabin, and Lane took possession of it and constructed a fence with a gate that Jenkins used to access the well. Lane put in a dispute to the territorial land office which was still unheard. Jenkins continued to use the remainder of the land. When the dispute arose, Lane put a lock on the gate and boasted around town that he would kill Jenkins if he attempted to use the well.

Naturally, Jenkins, after fortifying his courage with a swig or two of hootch, decided he would get water. He went unarmed to the gate with some armed friends, Ray Green and Henry Dufur. Jenkins broke the lock and entered. Lane confronted him and ordered him off the property. When he refused and proceeded to draw his water, Lane went to the cabin and returned with a shotgun.

As the tension mounted, Green attempted to fire on Lane, but the gun misfired. On hearing the click, Lane fired his shotgun directly at Jenkins. Jenkins died before he hit the ground. Green fired a second time, this time succeeded in wounding Lane in the leg.

The case was set to go before Judge Ladd, but Lane had engaged Tomas Ewing, a well-to-do lawyer and land speculator, to defend him. Sympathy seemed to be with Jenkins who left behind a widow and four children. He was a much respected man in his party. Still, it was clear Lane would prevail in the end.

The similarities to the ruse Lane had perpetrated on Dan earlier was troubling. Dan had succeeded in settling that dispute but not without several trips to Lecompton. It struck Dan that had Lane just been reacting to Green's attempted shot he would have fired at Green instead of Jenkins.

Becky interrupted his thoughts. "It looks good. All that wheat tossing in the breeze, doesn't it?"

Dan had not heard her approach. She was disheveled and sweaty in an old calico dress and smelled of herbs, dill and maybe some basil. She would not have looked better to him in silk and drenched with French perfume. "Yes, it was a good decision."

She came closer and slid her arm around his waist. "I have to get right back, but if you have a moment, I need a hand with the berry pot."

He remembered that today Becky was minding Dawn while André and Renee went into Lane City for some supplies. "I'm finished up here. Where is Dawn?"

"I bribed her to take a nap with the promise of a cookie when she wakes up."

"Well, we had better get back. If that little fireball wakes up, she may tear the cabin down looking for the cookie."

Dawn Rebecca Fitzgerald was still sound asleep when they entered the cabin. She lay curled with her thumb in her mouth. Her jet eyelashes brushed skin the color of parchment. The eyes they concealed were as green as her mother's while her light skin made her look as if she was André's natural offspring. Even in sleep, she was like a coiled spring. The child had more energy than two parents and an aunt and uncle could match combined. Becky studied the sleeping toddler with affection. "Renee will have her hands full when the new baby arrives."

Dan could see the wistfulness in Becky's eyes. They would both welcome a baby, but in spite of trying, it just hadn't happened yet. "I wonder if she will have this one on Thanksgiving Day," Dan commented.

"It's due around then," Becky agreed.

They turned their attention to the outside fireplace. It was just a small raised fireplace with a low chimney and had a clay bread oven. A delicious aroma emanated from the oven. Becky was making bread at the same time she was making preserves. The bread dough she had placed inside was calling to them through the closed oven door. She had built a hot fire in the oven then raked out the coals. The nice thing was that the residual heat in the clay baked the loaves while the original coals could be used for other cooking. In this case, the fire was being used to heat the large copper tub they usually used as a wash tub.

Today it was filled with a bubbling sugar and strawberry mixture. "As soon as it thickens just a little, I need you to help me take it off the fire so I can put the preserves in jars. Then as soon as it cools, I can seal it with the paraffin and we'll have strawberry preserves to eat all year long," Becky explained.

"I'll help on one condition," Dan said.

"And what is the condition?" she asked.

"I've got to have some of that preserves on the bread you are cooking. Soon. The smell is driving me crazy." Dan drew in a deep breath and fancied he could almost taste the bread slathered with the strawberry preserves. Becky and Renee had spent most Tuesday afternoons sharing their own special skills with the other. As a result, Renee now spoke like an educated New England lady and Becky cooked like someone who had spent years learning the art of Southern cooking.

"I'll even do better than that," Becky replied. "I churned up some fresh butter yesterday. It's sitting in the springhouse just waiting to meet up with fresh baked bread and strawberry preserves."

"Only one thing sounds sweeter than that." Dan leaned over and planted a soft kiss on her lips.

"Oh, You. Come on. Grab that handle and let's get this off the fire." Becky still blushed so nicely when he teased her.

"I'll wait until after dinner to explain just how you can satisfy my other sweet tooth." Dan gave a mock leer that left no doubt what he had in mind.

 Chapter 23

October 4, 1859—Lane City, Kansas Territory

Dan stopped to let Chieftain drink at the small branch off Pottawatomie Creek just before he entered Lane City. He was never comfortable in Lane City. Perhaps because it was named in honor of a man he disliked and mistrusted. The town had a prim Northern feel to it far different from the larger communities of Topeka and Lecompton. Usually, André came here if there was need of some supplies that could not wait for a trip into a larger town with a better stocked general store. Just a twitch of the reins started Chieftain back on the California Road headed into Lane City.

Today, the town's dirt main street was filled with wagons and horses. All the district's farmers were riding in to vote on one of the most important issues of the time, the Wyandotte Constitution. If approved, and Dan had no doubt it would be, it would then be presented to the United States legislature to vote on Kansas's admittance to statehood. This was the fourth constitution offered. The previous three had all been rejected by either the House, Senate or presidential veto. It was a liberal constitution, even permitting women to vote in school board elections and manage their own property, and naturally a free-state one. Jim Lane had referred to the Topeka Constitution as a "Blood Stained Banner," and for once Dan had agreed with his hated enemy. This final constitution had cost the blood of even more of Kansas citizens before coming to this point of a peaceful vote.

Dan exited the log building designated as the polling place after casting his vote in favor. "Howdy, Daniel," a cheerful voice hailed him.

Dan looked across the street at the door to the general store to see Thad Smith. Thad was an Ohioan who favored the Free-State party but was not a radical. He feared John Brown and did not trust Jim Lane at all. Thad ran the small store and the local post office. Dan felt comfortable with the man although Thad was really more André's friend. "Hello, Thad. How are you doing? I'm just headed over your way to get a cup of java."

"Doing well. How's your lovely wife and André's family?" André had deemed Lane City mostly a Free-State town safe to occasionally take Renee shopping to relieve the monotony of the tiny cabin.

Thad poured Dan a cup of strong black coffee from the white enamel pot he always kept on the edge of the hearth. "It's a good constitution we all can live with hopefully in peace from now on. Enough blood has been shed to decide this issue," Thad remarked.

"Far too much. I've been pushed into the fray to try and avenge what Brown did to my friends," Dan replied.

"What Osawatomie Brown did was awful, no doubt about it. I've never had personal issue that forced me to fight, but I don't approve of slavery. I can live in the states that already have it as a way of life. After all, General George Washington had slaves. I guess you have to accept the fact that it is the law and the constitution sanctions it. Still...."

"I guess you'll be voting for Robinson in the December election?" Dan steered the conversation into another direction.

"Indeed I will. Who gets your vote, Dan, Robinson or Medary?"

"I'm still on the fence. I like Medary's position on setting a fixed legal interest rate and providing land for common schools. Also I agree with him on preventing the forming of bogus banks dealing strictly in paper money with no foundation in gold or silver. Most of all, I like his recognition that the United States government is formed by the consent of individual states to enter into a union that is agreeable to all. We have to recognize that no one state or group of states can demand what another state needs to do."

Smith interrupted. "Still we need to preserve the union. Kansas will be a free and independent state able to govern itself within this union. I do think both candidates recognize that."

Dan continued, "On the other hand, Robinson has been here from the beginning and understands Kansas. He is strong enough to stand against Lane and offers a conservatism lacking in many Free-State party members. I believe his statement denying any connection to Brown's massacre of my friends."

Smith considered these points. " I think Robinson will win. Lane will be furious. Naturally, Lane will win a senate seat."

Dan grimaced. "Not with the help of my vote."

His coffee finished, Dan stood to take his leave of Thad. "I need to head back home. Can't leave all the work for André and the ladies."

"Wait. I think André has another letter waiting for him. I believe there is one for your wife, also. Let me get them for you."

Dan could think of no one André would be corresponding with, yet Thad seemed to think this was an ongoing exchange. *Strange.* He looked the letters over and saw no return address on the one addressed to André. Naturally Becky's was from her friend, Lydia Stone in

Lawrence. "Thanks, Thad, I'll give their letters to them as soon as I get home."

Several days later, Dan and André were finishing the sowing of their winter wheat crop when a neighbor, Adam Lancing, rode up to them. "Howdy Dan, André. I just got back from Topeka and thought you might want to hear the news, The votes are counted and the constitution is approved by a landslide. We're on our way to being a state."

"Thanks, neighbor. Want to sit a spell and have a cup of coffee?" Dan asked.

"Wish I could, but I need to get home. Got to finish up my planting. Looks like you boys are finished. Working two claims together looks like a good idea judging by what you are doing here."

"It works for us," André replied.

"Well, see ya." Lancing waved a hand and wheeled his horse back down the road.

Dan turned to André. "Guess we had better call it a day and head for our cabins. Want to go hunting next week? Wouldn't hurt to stock up on some meat before winter sets in."

"Sorry. I meant to mention it earlier, but I need to take off for a few weeks." André could not meet Dan's eyes. He always was a lousy liar.

"Must have slipped your mind, like that letter you were going to tell me all about a few days ago."

Dan had a hunch it was something dangerous, but he couldn't press André. When he freed his brother he knew that freedom involved making some dangerous choices. He had made a few near fatal ones, and André had stood by him. What could he say except "I'll keep an eye on Renee and the kids."

 Chapter 24

October 6, 1859—Pottawatomie Creek, Kansas Territory

After supper that night while she and Dan were sitting around the fireplace, Becky brought out her letter from Lydia. "Nathan attended the convention for that new Republican Party in Osawatomie. He added a page about the happenings. Would you like to hear what he has to say about the proceedings there?"

Dan settled closer to the blazing fire. He stretched his legs to take advantage of the warmth. "I sure would."

"Nathan says it was held at Samuel Greer's fine new two-story frame hotel that he built there after his old hotel was burned by Ruffians in the summer of '56.'" She stopped and cast a reproachful look at Dan. "I never told Lydia you took part in that attack."

Dan was unrepentant. "I'd do it again if I thought it was a chance to capture Ole Brown."

Becky continued perusing her letter. "Nathan says there were over five thousand people present in spite of the difficulty fording the over flowing steams and rain-soaked roads which were 'nigh on impassable' as he put it. And no, before you ask, John Brown was not present. Neither were Dr. Robinson or Jim Lane."

"No loss by not having Brown or Lane," Dan commented.

"I have to agree with you there," Becky said.

"He continues about how 'the party was divided with delegates ranging from raging abolitionists, who went so far as to give the right to vote to Negro men, to those 'black law' men, who wished all Negros banned from Kansas.'"

Dan interrupted. "Men like André would make more intelligent choices at the ballot box than people like Lane and Brown. It's the extremists on both sides causing the problems."

Becky returned to the letter in her hands. "Horace Greeley, Republican Party founder and New York Times editor, was a guest and Nathan was quite impressed with meeting him. 'Greeley spoke after the convention about political parties. He reviewed the old parties, the steady growth of the slave power and then dwelt on the origin, history, principles, and objects of the Republican party. He instructed the new Kansas Republican Party to be true to the ideals of freedom for all.'

Greeley also commented on all the tiny settlements springing up in Kansas. 'It seems it takes three log houses to make a city in Kansas, but you begin calling it a city so soon as they have staked out the lots.'"

"Amazing how many of these tiny settlements have grown in the past three years since André and I arrived here." Dan stirred the fire with the poker and added a log.

Becky concluded her review of Nathan's letter with, "'In spite of differences, Col. O. E. Learnard, convention president, kept the delegates fixed on the goal and they managed to draw up a platform and elect delegates to the Wyandotte Constitutional Convention to try and draw up yet another constitution. Again Neither Lane or Robinson was sent as delegates at that convention.'"

Becky folded the letter and returned it to the envelope. She began to prepare for bed. Dan followed her into the bedroom. "It's good to see reason beginning to prevail in Kansas. Even the Democrats at the Wyandotte Convention had dropped slavery from their platform. I was just discussing the Topeka Convention and constitution with Thad Smith. He's the postmaster and store owner in Lane City. You met him last time we went into town."

Becky nodded and Dan continued. "He is a Free-Stater, or I guess Republican is the right term now, and still is reasonable. There is hope all this will settle down and Kansas will become a nice peaceful state."

 Chapter 25

October, 1859—Pottawatomie Creek, Kansas Territory

André hated leaving Renee alone. He knew Dan already suspected that André had been acting as a conductor on the Underground Railroad for a while now. Since Dan and Becky were both crazy about Dawn and the new baby born on Thanksgiving day last year, Pilgrim Daniel, he knew the children would be well entertained.

He had only met John Brown the one time but was aware he was the mastermind behind the escape routes and plans. Dan could accept the idea of André helping runaways. He and Becky had helped conceal Renee. Still Dan felt an obligation to the Doyles to bring Brown to justice. It was a tangled mess, but André knew what he did was right. He and Dan might have a few words regarding André's involvement, albeit indirectly, with John Brown, but Dan would still look out for Renee and the babies while he was away.

This would be his longest trip. Since that first fateful night when he had to kill the slave hunter, he had made five trips. All were just overnighters to Prairie City. Still word of what he had done spread along that mysterious grapevine that made things known to slaves and their protectors that plantation owners and other whites rarely knew. He had built up quite a reputation: Runaways referred to him as Gabriel. Probably because Moses was already the code name of the most famous Negro conductor on the railroad, Harriet Tubman. He was scheduled to meet her and turn his "passengers" over to her in Chicago this trip. It would be the first time he had to go beyond Prairie City. John Armstrong had explained, "John Brown is involved with a secret mission, and I need to meet with him. You can stay at the Scales home and use the wagon."

At the cave, André looked over his charges. This time it was an entire family, the Jenkins. The man greeted him with a cautious "Hello, Gabriel."

"Hi, Jim. Glad to see ya'll are ready to travel. We'll have to be especially careful tonight as there are lots of troops and slave hunters around this area."

"We'un will make it. We done a'ready run all the way 'cross Missouri. Dey's gonna sell off my chillin. Ain't stayin' fo' dat to happen." The father was shivering in the cool night air. He had given the blanket to his wife. She was wrapped in it and the two children, a boy about eight and a girl around ten, huddled beneath another one.

The woman said nothing and jugged the blanket closer. It could not hide the fact that she was very pregnant. André debated trying to keep the family here until after the birth but decided it would not have made things easier to travel with an infant. He recalled the many times last year when baby Pilgrim had awakened them with a shrill shriek in the night. The thought decided him to push forward as fast as possible. "When is your baby due?" André asked.

Again it was Jim who spoke. "Matilda ain't gonna have dat baby 'til we in a free state."

André took another look at the woman's girth and hoped Jim was right.

The night went uneventfully. The children seemed to have unlimited energy, and even Matilda kept up with the rapid pace André set. Crossing the river was hard. Jim and André each carried a child and then went back to assist Matilda. They took off the blankets, rolled them in a bundle with André's coat and held them overhead while crossing the river. Still the lower part of the clothing got wet and the night was cold.

They stopped for the day at the Jones claim. Abigail and Wiley said they had been watched lately, so Wiley made his guests as comfortable as possible in a small smokehouse. They were able to dry out their clothes at a tiny fire that, in spite of their best efforts and leaving the door cracked, smoked them as if they were hams. At least they were dry.

They headed out at twilight. André felt the risk was worth the extra traveling time. When they arrived at the Scales home just after daybreak, again wet from fording streams and shivering with cold, they were treated to better accommodations. They gathered around the fireplace while Mrs. Scales prepared breakfast, and Negros and whites sat together at the dining room table and partook of a hearty meal. There was no caste at the Scales home. Caroline Scales and Sarah Armstrong petted the children and read them stories. The grownups talked of John Brown. Mrs. Scales remarked, "He looked bad last time I saw him. He had grown a beard as a disguise. It makes him look older."

Sarah broke in. "He sounded depressed too. At times he seemed almost manic. He acted like he knew he might never see us again."

André nodded. "Having such a large reward posted on your head could cause a man to be worried. He may be afraid of betrayal. President Buchanan has offered a two-hundred-fifty-dollar reward for John Brown's capture."

Mrs. Scales summed it up. "He is a bit strange sometimes, but he is a dear friend and we would protect him at any costs."

After breakfast the fugitives were hidden away in the cellar. André was given a spare room and allowed to sleep free of worry for his charges for a few hours. Two supportive neighbors, Mr. Ritchie and Mr. Sheridan, went into the town to solicit shoes and clothing for the runaways. André awoke refreshed that afternoon to find his little family newly clothed. Jim had been outfitted with a pair of denim overalls and a heavy flannel shirt. The children had been dressed in sturdy wool clothes and there was even a book with brightly colored pictures for each of them to take. Sarah had given all a brief first reading lesson, and the children were intrigued with the magic hidden in their precious books. The best that they had been able to do for Matilda was a thick woolen cape that barely covered her waistline.

At dusk the horses were hitched to the wagon, and the Jenkins except for Matilda hid in the secret compartment. Sarah Armstrong rode with them, and they pretended Matilda was her servant. André played the part of another slave whose job it was to drive his mistress. The sky was overcast, and the wind was cold and chilling. It was not a pleasant night for a journey, but considering Matilda's condition, they could not wait for better weather.

When the group reached the Kansas River, the ferry operator, Jacob Willits, took them to the other side. They did not stop for lunch as it was raining, just nibbled as they rode at some of the food Mrs. Scales had packed for them. They stopped for a cold supper at a pleasant clearing well shielded from the road by a row of trees later in the day when the rain stopped for a time. The children and Jim were happy for a chance to stretch their legs a bit.

As they were in a safer area inhabited mainly by people sympathetic to the runaways, they continued on in daylight. André napped for a short time while Sarah guided the team. They arrived in Holton around noon the following day, and the party took dinner at the Holton Hotel. They felt safer here as Holton had been founded by abolitionists from Milwaukee, Wisconsin. The town consisted of just a handful of homes, a sawmill, a blacksmith shop, a general store and the hotel. They continued on to the log house of Albert Fuller on Straight Creek, six miles northwest of Holton. It was a safe house to spend the night. The roads were bad on account of the rains, and the horses were exhausted. There, they were made welcome and a room prepared for Sarah and pallets fixed for André in the kitchen. The Jenkins were made comfortable in the cellar.

Just as André drifted off to sleep, there was a loud knock on the door. Mr. Fuller rushed from his bed dressed in long underwear and concealing a gun behind his back. André lay on his stomach and placed his gun beneath his chest. He feigned sleep.

Two young United States deputy marshals stood on the porch, their horses' reins looped over the porch rail. "Have you seen any slaves around here?" one of the men asked.

"Yes," said Fuller.

The marshals looked alert, and André gripped the gun tighter. *Could this be a trap?*

"My niece arrived today with her maid and a driver. Is there a problem?" Fuller looked so bemused, André had to smother a snicker.

Fuller's apparent honesty convinced the men there was no problem, and they rode away.

André almost choked he was laughing so hard. "Boy, you played that well. Almost convinced me you were just an honest law-abiding man who would turn in the first runaway you saw."

"Go back to sleep. You're safe here." Fuller yawned and went back to bed as if fending off U. S. Marshals was nothing new.

Sarah bid them all goodbye here and returned to Kansas. André let the group and horses rest until late in the day. He knew it would be safer traveling at night after they left the vicinity of Holton. The rain had cleared, and traveling was faster. They reached the Elihu Whittenhall log cabin near Albany just before dawn. The family made them welcome, but the cabin was crowded with Elihu and his wife and four boisterous daughters. The Jenkins children enjoyed having other children with whom to romp and play. Mrs. Whittenhall entertained them by playing on a beautiful piano they claimed was the only one of its kind in Kansas Territory. André was restless thinking of his own two children at home and hoping he made it safely back to them and Renee. He had been told the next leg of the trip—crossing into Nebraska—was going to be rough, but he had no idea how challenging it would prove to be. Matilda was restless. Jim was the only member of the party who seemed to sleep soundly.

They departed just at twilight. Elihu and a neighbor, William Graham, rode with them to help get the party across the Big and Little Nemaha Rivers. Elihu would have felt safer putting the entire Jenkins family in the secret compartment of the wagon, but Matilda would not fit so they disguised her instead. She was dressed in a black mourning dress. long gloves to hide her hands and a hat with a heavy dark veil that covered her face completely. The cover story if they were stopped would be that André was the driver and William Graham, who wore a black armband, his owner. Matilda was his wife who was too grief-stricken over the loss of her father to speak. They had to ford the Big Nemaha River, and the ride was bumpy but accomplished with not too much trouble. The ferry at Little Nemaha was operated by a William Finney, a known abolitionist, so no problem was expected there or the rest of the way to Nemaha City. Elihu and William left them and borrowed horses from Mr. Finney to return home.

Problems have a way of cropping up when not expected. This trip was no exception. André had just driven off the ferry when he heard a loud moan from the wagon.

He stopped and opened the passenger door. Matilda was half lying across the front seat. She had pulled the hat and veil off and looked troubled. "Are you all right?" André asked.

"Yessa, but I think my baby gonna come anytime now." She sounded frightened.

André was frightened for a different reason. He had no idea how to deliver a baby. He helped Jim out from the secret compartment and asked, "Can you deliver a baby?"

"Lorwdy, nosiree. The mistress or some o' the other women in the quarter al'ays done he'p with dat. I jest figure when dat chile ready to come into this worl' he comin' no matter what."

André made a decision. He hoped it was the right one. "Get in the wagon with your wife and hold her hand, talk to her, whatever you can think of. I'm going to race this rig full chisel for Squire Kennedy's house."

Jim was reluctant to get in the wagon. "Maybe I oughta stay under heah wit' bub and sis. I do'n rightly know what I kin do to he'p?"

"You can pray," André replied as he jumped back on the seat and grabbed the whip.

By the time he pulled up at the Kennedy home, André thought he had made the best time of the entire trip these last few miles. He jumped down and pounded on the door. It was still dark, and all the lamps were off inside. An older man quickly answered his knocking, and André shouted, "Mr. Kennedy, I have a woman giving birth in that wagon."

Kennedy threw open the door. "Get her in. I'll roust up my wife."

When Jim and André brought Matilda inside, a sleepy looking lady took charge. "Put her in there." She indicated a small room off the kitchen with a cot and a wash pail. "Now go. Shoo. She made a motion toward Jim and André as if chasing chickens from her garden. André turned to make a more formal introduction to his host while Jim retrieved the children from the wagon.

The children played in the front room near the fireplace while Kennedy offered Jim and André some of the family's last night's supper. Cold bacon and hominy washed down with a steaming cup of coffee never tasted so good. Jim paced back and forth while André and

Kennedy talked about crops, the weather and how much longer the trip might take. They all tried to ignore the screams that came from the little room.

After several hours, an even more disheveled Mrs. Kennedy came into the room. She gave a Jim an accusing look. "Congratulations, you are a father again. You may go in to your wife now."

"Is it a boy or a girl?" Jim asked as he rushed across the room.

It might have been a twinkle in the crusty old lady's eye. Or then maybe André imagined it. She turned and headed back to her bedroom. "You'll be surprised."

Jim returned to the room a huge grin on his face and a bundle in each arm."We dun got twins. A boy and a girl. One of each. Watya think o' that?"

André's first thought was that it made the remainder of the journey doubly dangerous, but he could not squash Jim's natural elation."

"We's in Nebraska, right?" Jim asked.

"Yes, you are," André replied.

"Do it be a free or slave state?" Jim continued.

Kennedy answered this time. "We're still a territory, and slavery has not been legally abolished here yet, but there are only about ten slaves in the whole territory. A law abolishing slavery in this territory is before the legislature now. It's only a matter of time until we pass it."

Jim turned to André with an I-told-you-so look. "Hallalula. Dese babies been born free."

He brought his wife a bit of the cold food, but she was too worn out to eat. When Jim returned to the room, he looked at André. "We gonna name these babies for yo' and Moses. Without you two they would'a been born slaves. They be named André and Harriet.

That evening, Kennedy advised André to move his charges to the next stop, the Mayhew cabin. "It's safer. In fact, you could stay a few days to give Matilda chance to recuperate as there is a well-hidden cave underground there."

Allen Mayhew and his wife Barbara Kagi Mayhew greeted André and his passengers warmly. Barbara was the sister of John Kagi, one of John Brown's closest associates. About twenty-five feet from the cabin Allen and his brother-in-law had created a dugout cave which was reached by a tunnel from a nearby ravine. The entrance was well hidden by brush and small trees. The cave was about ten by twelve feet and furnished with blankets, pallets and a table. It was as safe as any place in the country could be for a runaway slave.

The Mayhews hid the wagon behind the house and stabled the horses in their barn. They invited André into the cabin and left the

Jenkins to have a little much needed privacy to get acquainted with their new offspring.

The cottonwood log cabin was one room with a loft above for sleeping. Although small, it was cozily furnished with a wood stove, a colorful chest for storage that could also be used for seating, a table and a handmade bed with a patchwork quilt. A calendar displayed an advertisement for farm implements and reminded André that today was already October nineteenth. He had been away from home for a week already. The Mayhew children, Edward, Henry, Charles and Thomas, ranging from ten-year old Edward to one-year old Thomas, were promised they could play with the Jenkins children when the adults brought breakfast to the cave. The baby, Thomas, was around the same age as André's Pilgrim. He was playing with a red and blue Jacob's Ladder. The toddler kept nudging the toy to make it move and then laughing at the simple toy. It made André miss his own children intensely.

Mrs. Mayhew prepared a huge breakfast with cornmeal, eggs, bacon and biscuits for the Jenkins. Allen and André, accompanied by the three older boys, brought it to the cave. Matilda had recovered her appetite and promised to give good shrift to her share. Jim and Matilda were both happy to learn it would be safe to remain here a few days. The cave, with its hidden entrance, made them feel secure, and the small space they could share as a family was as close to a home as they had ever had before — on the plantation their cabin was larger and better furnished, but it had to be shared with another family.

That night André was settled in the loft with the boys. He had already told them a story about a brave little boy who outsmarted an evil ogre and saved his village. He tensed when he heard the sound of a horseman galloping toward the cabin. He put his fingers to his lips in the universal sign for quiet to the boys, and giggling, they compiled, thinking it went along with the earlier story. André leaned as close as he could to the edge of the loft. He heard Allen open the door and greet a neighbor. Still, André didn't let down his guard. It was very late for a social call. He only heard snippets of the conversation. "John Brown," "Harpers Ferry," "Brother-in-law killed."

He heard the door close and the rider begin to gallop away. Allen had answered the door, but apparently Mrs. Mayhew had heard the entire conversation. She screamed, "No! No! Not John Henry."

André hated to intrude on a private family scene, but he had heard enough to know this was more than just a personal tragedy. He had to know more. He climbed down the ladder to see Allen holding his sobbing wife."What happened?"

Allen handed him a folded newspaper. "Her brother, John Henry

Kagi, was killed while helping John Brown attempt a slave revolt at Harpers Ferry."

André skimmed the article then reread it more carefully. John Brown along with sixteen white men, four free Negros and one fugitive slave and holding nine hostages, had attacked the arsenal at Harpers Ferry, Virginia. He had barricaded his men in a small engine house. Northern abolitionist groups had sent him a hundred ninety-eight breech loading .52 caliber Sharp's carbines similar to Dan's called "Beecher's Bibles," and he had ordered a blacksmith to create nine hundred fifty pikes modeled on the Bowie knife he had taken from Captain Pate. The same one that had almost cost Dan his leg.

The arsenal contained a hundred thousand muskets and rifles. Brown attempted to attract more Negro recruits. He tried recruiting Frederick Douglass as a liaison officer to the slaves. Douglass declined, telling Brown the raid was "a suicide mission." Still Brown felt he could arm rebellious slaves by gathering recruits as he marched first through Virginia and eventually into the heart of the deep South.

Brown had cut the telegraph wire and captured a train passing through. Then for unknown reasons, he let the train continue and naturally alert the authorities. President James Buchanan ordered a contingent of U.S. Marines to Harpers Ferry under the command of Brevet Colonel Robert E. Lee of the 2nd U.S. Cavalry. Lee sent his aide, Lt. J.E.B. Stuart, under a flag of truce to negotiate a surrender of John Brown. He told the marine commander, Lt. Greene, if Brown refused, he was to lead the marines in storming the engine house. Stuart confronted Brown and informed him that he and his men would be spared if they surrendered. Brown refused, saying, "I would rather die here."

Brown and six of his men were captured. Eleven, including John Henry Kagi and two of Brown's sons, Watson and Owen, were killed. Four men escaped and were being hunted.

Colonel Lee stated he believed Brown was insane.

André's first thought was *My God! What a waste of lives. His cause was just, but his mind was deranged to believe he could get away with something like this.* His next thought was *this is going to make the Jenkins' escape even harder. Every slave hunter and Southern fire-eater is now up in arms.*

 Chapter 26

October 1859—Iowa

Knowing the last leg of this trip could hold unpleasant surprises, André herded his charges back into the wagon at twilight and crossed into Iowa. No one from the Mayhew house accompanied them, so there was no "Massa-Slave" cover story if he were stopped. Luck rode with them tonight. They had pushed hard and not stopped for meals.

Their first stop in Iowa was at Reverend John Todd's modest frame home near Tabor. André had been told that the entire town was strongly abolitionist, so they were safe unless any parties of slave hunters or federal marshals were roaming about. Todd fed them and offered a small secret room for them to rest. He showed André where he had stored an arsenal of Sharp's rifles in the cellar and a small cannon in his barn for John Brown's recent venture. "I had no idea what he planned to use them for or I would have done differently," Todd assured André.

Confident of their relative safety they slept well for a few hours. André decided to strike out for their next stop while still daylight. The farther he got the Jenkins from any guns connected to Harper's Ferry, the safer he felt.

This time they moved northward paralleling the Nebraska-Iowa border to Council Bluff. Their safe house here was the home of a middle-class commodities trader named John Williamson. The candle in the front window and a quilt hanging across the porch rail let them know it was safe to stop.

The door was thrown open at the first tap of the knocker. André found himself facing a striking looking man who appeared to be of mixed Negro and Indian blood. "John Williamson. Welcome to my home." The stranger extended his hand.

He made the travelers feel welcome and offered them the security of his attic where the group dined and rested until twilight. When they made ready to leave, Williamson presented Jim and Matilda with some forged manumission papers. "Don't put too much faith in them, but they do give you a shot if you get hauled before a friendly magistrate."

They reached the large stone home of Rev. George Hitchcock, another Congregational Minister, just after daybreak. Sure enough, there were three white bricks piled near the front door, the signal that this was the right place. The home was the most elegant they had visited so far, two full stories and built of limestone blocks. Rev. Hitchcock welcomed André and the Jenkins. "I was worried about you. I heard the news about Brother Brown."

"Yes, Rev, we were at his sister's home several days ago, and she took the news hard."

"I'll pray for her and Brother Allen as well. I cannot condone what Brother Brown did, but he did it to further his cause. Only God can decide if it was a sin or not." The preacher looked fondly at the older Jenkins children. "Your children must be exhausted. I was told two children. No one mentioned the babies."

Jim spoke up. "Our twins be newborn. Born in freedom. Praise the Lord and thank ya Rev. for he'ping us."

"A true Christian could not stand by and see people enslaved. You must be tired and hungry. Let me show you to the basement. You'll be safe there."

He led them through an elegant room with wallpaper and rugs on the wide plank floor and down a stairwell to a spacious basement. Along one wall were a bank of shelves filled with blankets and supplies. He moved the shelves and revealed a hidden door. Inside the secret room was a large sleeping area with a soft stuffed ticking and heavy quilts, chairs and a washstand. A lantern hung from the low exposed timber ceiling. Solid posts supported the weight of the house above. The room was spacious with no windows and walled with solid limestone blocks that allowed no sound or light to escape and give away its secret. André knew he would sleep better here than in one of the fancy guest rooms upstairs. The minister left with a cheerful "I'll hide your wagon behind the house and be back with some food shortly."

The door had been left slightly ajar to let a little fresh air into the room. The travelers were all hungry, so when they had washed up, they gathered near the door to await their meal. André thought he heard the sound of several horses but could not be sure because of the room's construction. He was instantly alert when he heard the sound of pounding on the home's front door. Matilda was nursing the twins, and the children were playing quietly farther into the room. Jim stepped up behind André and nodded, making André aware he also heard the commotion upstairs. Both men were poised for fight or flight should the occasion arise, but if an armed posse descended and located the room, there would be no way out. André doubted the fake papers Williamson had procured for the Jenkins would convince anyone.

André eased the door so only a crack was left to permit the two men to listen to the upstairs conversation. The voices were muted, but André could make out a few words clearly. "Looking for runaways… ,"demanded a rough voice.

Rev. Hitchcock's calm answer calmed the men. "None here, but do come in. You are welcome to look around. I am sinfully proud of my new home."

The visitors must have been offered coffee as there was a little time when no words were heard. Then there were footsteps above. Hitchcock was leading his guests through the home. Finally a loud squeaking as the men began to descend the steps to the basement. One of the men commented, "You need a few nails to fix those squeaking steps."

The minister replied, "Just haven't gotten around to that yet."

André smiled. Hitchcock managed to avoid a direct lie even in these circumstances. He had no doubt the good reverend had deliberately fixed the stairs to squeak as a warning to anyone below. He silently eased the door closed and, as a precaution, extinguished the lantern, after signaling the others to be quiet.

They all waited in the dark for what seemed like an eternity. Suddenly the door was pushed open. André held his breath, but it was only the minister holding a laden tray. "I always make my guests feel welcome and show off my home so they never feel I am hiding anything. No one has ever discovered this room. Enjoy and rest well."

They all murmured their thanks. Hitchcock left them to their meal and some much needed rest.

For this part of their journey, there were no safe houses for the next two nights, so André picked secluded spots where he could pull the wagon deep into the woods. They rested most of each day and took to the road again as darkness descended. He was not sure how well the Jenkins' fake papers, or even his own legitimate ones, would work if cornered by a rabid slave hunter being paid for each slave he recaptured. Several times each day they heard hooves of carriages on the road but no one discovered their hiding place.

Their next station was the home of a James Jordan, known as the "Chief Conductor." The house was huge and quite elaborate. The owner greeted them and announced, "Just call me Uncle Jimmy."

He had a decidedly Southern accent which he explained came from growing up in the west part of Virginia. "I was on the other side of this issue when I was a young man. My family were slaveholders."

"What changed you?" André asked.

"A very sad story. I'll tell you all about it while we dine."

He led them down to the basement where the kitchen was located. A strong looking woman, whom he introduced as his wife, Melinda, was stirring a pot at the wood stove.

The children were sent to eat with Jordan's own large brood. Matilda set the twins down on a well-padded quilt to sleep. The adults settled around a sturdy oak table. "Forgive the lowly accommodations instead of our dining room, but this is safer if not as elegant," Jordan apologized.

André had forgotten how elaborate Southern manners were. He opted for safety over elegance nowadays. The hearty stew was delicious, and the fresh baked bread crispy as Jordan told the promised tale. "I was a young'un about nineteen or so when I was recruited to join a party to help search for some runaways from a neighboring plantation. These people had a poor reputation among most of the neighborhood gentry, but still it was the neighborly thing to do." He paused to slather his bread with the fresh butter. "There were dogs running around, and finally they caught a scent. We followed the howls and found some of the runaways, a mother and two children, hiding in a thicket. Her clothing was torn, and she held a baby not much bigger than your twins." He gestured toward the sleeping pair of infants. "The little boy, about the same age as your youngest fellow, clung to his mother's arm."

"Many runaways are captured before they get very far," André commented.

"Yes. But it made a strong impression on me. I have never forgotten that woman's eyes looking up at me from the bushes."

"Did she be sent back to her owner?" Jim asked.

"Unfortunately, yes."

"That be awful." Matilda murmured with a sidelong glance to assure herself her own twins still were safe. "I rather die than go back."

"You are not going back," André assured her.

"Danged right," Jordan added.

"Wat happen'd ta that woman?" Jim asked.

"She and her children were my first passengers on the Railroad. She made it to Canada, and so have all my other passengers."

Matilda had tears in her eyes when Melinda Jordan led her, Jim and their children upstairs to their bedroom. André stayed behind with James Jordan."Would you care to see some of my newest stock?" Jordan asked.

"Love to. I come from Louisiana where prize horses and racing is one of the favorite pastimes among the gentry. Not that I took part in the activities, but I sure did admire the horses."

"Did you run?" Jordan asked.

"No." André told an abbreviated version of how he gained his freedom, omitting his relationship with Dan.

"Your Dan sounds like a good man. I'd like to meet him one day."

"You're welcome to visit whenever you come our way. I know Dan would like to meet another Southerner who feels the way he does about slavery, not to mention a fellow horse lover," André answered.

Jordan had led the way to a large corral with about a dozen horses, but a big gray stallion in a pen by himself caught André's eye. "How come that fellow is penned all by himself? Is he a maverick?"

Jordan nodded his head. "He sure is. Handsomest horse in the lot but won't respond to reining. Wild as a bedbug. He's broken and understands reining just won't respond like he should. Won't let anyone handle him unless he is roped and tied, and then he still fights like the dickens. My foreman is talking of gelding him, but I hate to do that to such a specimen."

They walked over to the pen. The big gray pawed the ground and rolled his eyes at the two men. He sidestepped farther away. André could see whip marks on his withers. In spite of knowing the horse was way out of his price range, André had to ask. "How much you want for him?"

"He's probably worth about two hundred dollars or so. I bought him as part of a lot. Still if a body can't ride him, he's not worth a plugged nickel." Jordan looked from André to the horse. "Go on, see if you can handle him."

André stepped back to a feed bag and took a handful of grain. H climbed over the fence and approached the gray, trying to maintain eye contact all the while. The horse continued to sidestep away and reared slightly. André ignored the movements and steadily continued his approach. He began speaking in a soft tone. "Hi, boy. Don't you want a little feed? I won't hurt you. Just want to be friends." He continued in a soft monotone until the horse became still and finally cautiously approached and accepted the grain from him. André held the horse's silky mane and leapt on his back. He held himself low and clamped his legs around the horse's middle and kept his heels low and tight on the animal's sides. He let the horse run a little and then slowed him by gripping the mane and pulling back a little. He turned his head toward James Jordan and the horse trotted that way. André slid down and gave the big stallion a friendly pat on his withers. "Good boy."

"Well, I'll be danged." Jordan scratched his head. "Tell ya' what. Since the danged animal is almost useless to me and he seems to have taken to you, you can have him for twenty-five dollars. I'll throw in an old saddle and some tack, and you can tie him behind the wagon on your way back to Topeka and then have a way to ride home."

"You got yourself a deal, Mr. Jordan. I feel I am taking advantage of you, however. The horse is just afraid of a saddle and needs to be trained back to one gently, not with a whip."

"Good luck with the training." Jordan stuck out a hand. "We got a deal?"

André shook and dug in his wallet for the money before Jordan changed his mind. "We do indeed."

He walked back to the pen and offered the gray another handful of grain. "We are going to be partners, Silver."

"Hate to break up your love fest, but we will be having a guest arrive any minute. Mrs. Tubman, or should I say "Moses," will be here soon to take over your passengers," Jordan said.

The two men returned to the house and lit up a pair of cigars. Talk turned back to the Jenkins."I'll miss them. We have become almost like family traveling so far together. Still I am glad that the heavy responsibility is lifted from my shoulders. It's been scary," André said.

"I know how you feel." The two men smoked in companionable silence until a knock roused them. "Stay here. If it's not someone safe, I'll not let them into the house, but if I am forced, use the back door," Jordan indicated the passageway, "and hide in the barn right out back. Get down under some hay."

André listened for any sounds of danger and heard only a warm greeting and a husky woman's voice. He prepared himself for a tall stately well-dressed woman. Instead, Jordan issued in a shabby small woman in clothes more appropriate to a kitchen maid than this renowned supporter of freedom. When she spoke, he forgot her small stature and shabby clothes. "Greetings, André, or should I call you 'Gabriel'? Your fame has spread."

"Just André, and I am truly honored to meet you, Moses."

Her deep laugh rang out. "We all have a destiny to live up to. You have done well on your first long run."

"The Jenkins have become like family to me. I could not place them in better hands."

"Oh, I'll get them to safety. I haven't lost a passenger yet," she replied.

"Do you have any advice for a novice, ma'am?" André asked.

"You have to be ruthless sometimes," she replied.

"How do you mean?" André assumed she was referring to fighting slave hunters.

"Never risk your entire party for one person." Tubman explained. "If any of my passengers get cold feet, I remind them, a live runaway can do great harm by going back, but a dead one can tell no secrets."

Since he was able to travel freely, André made good time on the return trip. When he returned the wagon and bid goodbye to John Armstrong, André eased a saddle on Silver's back and a bit between his teeth. "I know you don't like this much, big boy, but I promise I will take it easy until you get used to it."

Silver pranced a little but submitted. André had already won his trust with frequent apples, carrots and generous petting. Astride, André held the reins loosely. He guided the animal more with his legs and by turning his head in the direction he wished to go than by using the reins which seemed to hurt Silver's sensitive mouth. He gave Silver his head, and the horse ate up the miles back home at a good pace.

André was already in the barn grooming Silver when Dan opened the door. "Welcome home, wanderer," Dan commented.

He stepped into the barn and saw Silver. "Wow! That animal is as fine as cream gravy."

André gave the glossy white coat one more brush. "That he is. And I got him for a song."

"Okay, what is wrong with him?" Dan asked.

"Not a thing anymore. He was a bit saddle shy, but he and I have come to an understanding."

Dan looked at his brother's satisfied smile. "I suppose you are going to tell me you were on a horse buying trip?"

"You might say that. Among other things."

Dan persisted. "I suppose you don't want to tell me about the 'other things'?"

"You suppose right. What you don't know can't hurt you."

"If one can believe rumors I have heard, you are considered something of an angel by certain passengers of a secret train."

"Still if I ever get caught, you can't be dragged into court and made to testify to rumors."

Dan reached over and patted his brother's back. "I hope the day never comes when you get caught. You know I will always stand by you no matter what."

"I hope the day comes when I won't have to do this anymore."

Dan changed the subject. "I got a letter from Mrs. Doyle a few days ago. She asked about all of our health and enclosed a copy of a letter she sent to John Brown in prison. Want to read it?"

André nodded, and Dan passed a much-folded piece of paper to him. André opened it and began to read.

> *Chattanooga Tennessee 20th November 1859*
> *John Brown*
> *Sir*
> *Altho vengeance is not mine, I confess, that I do feel*
> *gratified to hear that you ware stopt in your fiendish*
> *career at Harper's Ferry, with the loss of your two sons,*
> *you can now appreciate my distress, in Kansas, when you*
> *then and there entered my house at midnight and arrested*
> *my husband and two boys and took them out of the yard*
> *and in cold blood shot them dead in my hearing, you*
> *cant say you done it to free our slaves, we had none and*
> *never expected to own one, but has only made me a poor*
> *disconsolate widow with helpless children while I feel*
> *for your folly. I do hope & trust that you will meet your*
> *just reward. O how it pained my Heart to hear the dying*
> *groans of my Husband and children if this scrawl give*
> *you any consolation you are welcome to it.*
> *my son John Doyle whose life I begged of (you) is now*
> *grown up and is very desirous to be at Charleston on*
> *the day of your execution would certainly be there if his*
> *means would permit it, that he might adjust the rope*
> *around your neck if gov: wise would permit it*
> *Mahala Doyle*

André looked up after reading the letter. "I sincerely hope she finds peace on John Brown's death. Strangely enough, I hope Brown finds peace then too. Most of all I hope our country finds peace."

 Chapter 27

December 1859—Leavenworth, Kansas Territory

Dan and André rode toward Leavenworth, Dan on Chieftain and André on a well-behaved Silver. That strange lawyer from Illinois, whom many members of the brand new Republican Party said would be the next president, was speaking there today. Although André naturally could not vote, he was just as interested in what the so-called "rail splitter" had to say.

In spite of the bitter cold and icy covered ground, the city was crowded with visitors who had come to hear the speech and get a glimpse of the speaker. It was a city, no longer just a frontier town. The streets were lined with many stone buildings mingled with the older frame ones. Shops of every kind abounded. Dan reminded himself to pick out a nice Christmas present for Becky while here. He had no doubt André would also find something special for Renee.

Lincoln was staying at the Mansion House, which was jokingly referred to as "Abolition Hotel" because of the sentiments of its owners. Dan and André arrived in time to see a parade of several carriages and wagons with a band playing loudly. A clean-shaven man stepped out of a carriage and ascended the steps of the hotel. He was tall and gaunt, dressed in ill-fitted clothing and had a buffalo robe around his shoulders. John C. Vaughan, editor of the Leavenworth Times, welcomed Lincoln to Leavenworth. Lincoln said a few gracious words and proceeded into the hotel accompanied by friends, local lawyer Mark Delahay, among them.

André voiced what both were thinking. "That barrow-tram is the controversial 'Honest Abe' that everybody is talking about?"

"He does look like he was rode hard and put up wet," Dan confirmed.

The two brothers shook their heads and proceeded down the street. They were staying the night at the Planters Hotel, owned by Northerners Len T. Smith and Col. Jepp Rice who tried to appeal to both parties. In fact they even hired two bartenders, one pro-slavery, the other Free-State. When a thirsty Southerner would begin drinking and between drinks proceed to give vent to his opinion on matters of importance, he immediately found an interested listener and sympathizer in the person of the Southern barkeep. When a Free-State man did the same and voiced contrary opinions, he found a kindred soul in the barkeeper at the other end of the bar.

The desk clerk took their money quickly and handed them a key. "Room 222. Jest up them stairs."

Their room faced the river and was clean and comfortable. There was a copy of the *Leavenworth Times* sitting on the washstand. André picked it up. "Something we both are interested in here."

"What's that?" Dan asked.

"John Brown was executed yesterday. They have his last speech in here." André perused the newspaper.

"Well, maybe the Doyles can rest easy now. At least I kept my word to Mrs. Doyle and attempted to avenge her menfolks."

André read aloud a part of Brown's statement: 'I believe that to have interfered as I have done—as I have always freely admitted I have done—in behalf of His despised poor, was not wrong, but right. Now, if it is deemed necessary that I should forfeit my life for the furtherance of the ends of justice, and mingle my blood further with the blood of my children and with the blood of millions in this slave country whose rights are disregarded by wicked, cruel, and unjust enactments,—I submit; so let it be done!' He is making himself a martyr with this speech."

"Martyr, balderdash! He was a bad egg to begin with, and it's high time they bedded him down. I'm only sorry I didn't get a shot at him first."

"Whoa. Danny Boy. No point getting your Irish up. It's over now."

Dan felt relieved in a way. It was over. Or at least he hoped it was. André's comment about Brown being considered a martyr rankled. He just knew that wasn't possible. No one would admire a murderer like Brown. *Or will they?* a tiny voice in his mind murmured.

That night Stockton Hall was packed. The building was large, made of stone and housed shops on the ground floor. The upstairs hall was fitted out elaborately. The building was well-lighted and heated and had plush armchair seating. André and Dan had managed to find good seats. When the Illinois lawyer took the stage, the house became instantly quiet. As expected he spoke about Kansas's impending statehood. "You, the people of Kansas, furnish the example of the first application of this new policy. At the end of about five years, after having almost continual struggles, fire and bloodshed, over this very question, and after having framed several State Constitutions, you have, at last, secured a Free State Constitution, under which you will probably be admitted into the Union."

Dan murmured to André, "I'll bet the fact that Kansas will have six electoral votes in the presidential election might have a little something to do with his being here tonight."

André nodded his agreement. Lincoln continued. He drove home the Republican platform that while they did not approve of slavery expanding, they did not intend to interfere with the rights of the slave states. "We are not trying to destroy it. The peace of society and the structure of our government both require that we should let it alone, and we insist on letting it alone. If I might advise my Republican friends here, I would say to them, leave your Missouri neighbors alone. Have nothing whatever to do with their slaves. Have nothing whatever to do with the white people, save in a friendly way. Drop past differences, and so conduct yourselves that if you cannot be at peace with them, the fault shall be wholly theirs."

This time it was André who commented. "He's trying to straddle both sides of that rail fence. He doesn't want to anger the Southern states any more than they are already"

Lincoln made the politician's mandatory connection with the founding fathers."The Fathers did not seek to interfere with slavery where it existed but to prevent its extension. This was the policy of the Republican party of today." He ended with a warning to Southern states. "If we shall constitutionally elect a President, it will be our duty to see that you submit. Old John Brown has been executed for treason against a State. We cannot object, even though he agreed with us in thinking slavery wrong. That cannot excuse violence, bloodshed and treason. It could avail him nothing that he might think himself right. So, if we constitutionally elect a President, and therefore you undertake to destroy the Union, it will be our duty to deal with you as old John Brown has been dealt with. We shall try to do our duty. We hope and believe that in no section will a majority so act as to render such extreme measures necessary."

On the walk back to the hotel, Dan commented, "The man is an impressive speaker and sounds reasonable, but Seward had the edge and I think that is who will get the nomination."

"I would not be too sure," André replied. "These are strange and strained times."

 Chapter 28

New Year's Day 1860—Pottawattamie Creek, Kansas Territory

Becky awoke early on New Year's Day. She put on her best dress and added her favorite Christmas present, the lovely ivory brooch Dan had brought her from Leavenworth. It went so beautifully with her cherished ivory combs her grandfather had made for her long ago. She arranged them in her hair using the mirror Dan had also bought her. Her reflection showed much the same face she had seen every morning in Lawrence before she met Dan. What it didn't show was the great happiness she had in her husband and well-ordered if simple home. It couldn't reflect the fear she had each time Dan rode out on Chieftain with his Sharp's rifle, Little Thunder, set in its scabbard. What a silly custom she thought for men to name their rifles. Too, that reflection did not show her deepest regret, that she and Dan had no children. She loved Dawn and little Pill, as Dawn insisted on calling her brother. The name had stuck, and now no one ever called the toddler Pilgrim.

Dan entered with a bucket of fresh milk and a basket of eggs. "I fed all the stock," he called out.

From the bedroom door, Becky watched as he carefully laid the eggs on the table and sat the bucket next to her churn. He went back outside and reentered with another bucket before he took off his old coat. "I got up really early, so I went down to the creek and got you a big batch of those mapleleaf mussels you like so much."

She flew over and planted a kiss on his lips. "Thank you. You know how I miss my New England Clam Chowder, and that recipe Renee worked out for me is so much like it. We'll have some for dinner today."

"Girl, you keep kissing me like that, we won't have time for dinner today."

"Oh you." Becky blushed.

Dan let go of her waist and patted her fanny. "I guess we had better put a hold on the kissing. I saw André at the barn, and he and Renee will be over as soon as she gets the kids dressed. He said she made a special Leap Year Cake since this will be a leap year."

"Wonderful! She is such a great cook. She taught me so much."

"In return, you helped her speak more correctly," Dan added.

"She is a quick learner." Becky tied an apron over her good dress. "I had better get the turkey on the spit."

Renee and the children were inside. Renee was helping Becky finish up the last-minute preparations for dinner. Dawn was playing with the corncob doll Becky had made for her as a Christmas present. André led Dan outside. "The women have it all under control. I need a breath of fresh air."

Dan followed. "Good idea."

Once on the porch they settled into two hickory limb chairs. Mason and Dixon settled in at their feet. André reached inside his coat and brought out an envelope. "Remember that letter I got back in October?"

Dan nodded.

André continued. "I appreciate you respecting my privacy enough not to pry, but I want to tell you about it."

"We've always been able to talk about anything." Dan absently scratched Dixon's neck.

"It was from your father...."

Dan jumped to his feet and opened his mouth to shout, driving both dogs off the porch.

"Whoa. Danny Boy, calm down," André said. "I've been writing to him to keep in touch with my mother. I miss her and Sallie, you know. Him too, truth be told."

Dan sank back into the chair. "Go on."

"I'd be lying if I told you we never discussed you. He understands how you feel about the situation. He gave things a lot of thought after you left. He freed my mother and sister and has made provisions for them in his will in case of his death."

The thought of his powerful father dying had never occurred to Dan. "He's too mean to die."

"We can all die at any time. You with your fighting to avenge the Doyles' death. Me with, well I guess you know what I have been doing lately."

Dan nodded. "I understand. I hate slavery too."

André continued. "Anyway, he gave me a letter for you and asked me to give it to you when the time was right. I'm not sure there will ever be a right time, but here it is." He held out the envelope.

Dan shook his head. "I do have a bit more understanding about that fine line between right and wrong, but I can't forgive him."

"I'm not asking that. Just take the letter, and when you feel the time is right, open it and read what he has to say."

Dan reached out and took the envelope. He tucked it into his coat pocket as if it were a poisonous snake coiled to strike. "I can't promise I will ever be ready to communicate with him again, but I will keep the letter. Maybe one day I will read it."

"Fair enough," André replied.

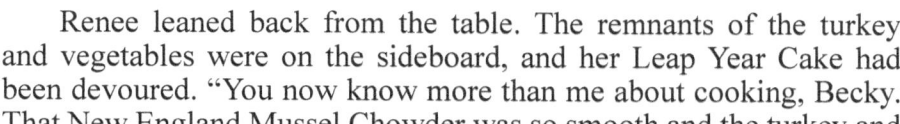

Renee leaned back from the table. The remnants of the turkey and vegetables were on the sideboard, and her Leap Year Cake had been devoured. "You now know more than me about cooking, Becky. That New England Mussel Chowder was so smooth and the turkey and vegetables perfect."

"Thanks to you—I owe it all to you. When I came here I had never cooked anything more complex than toast. Your bread and that cake. Oh that cake. I've never tasted anything more delicious." Becky had eaten more than her share.

Dan poured them each a glass of plum wine Renee and Becky had made from the wild plums the year Renee had arrived in their midst. "I'd like to propose a toast to the two best women in Kansas Territory."

André raised his glass and tapped their rims. "I agree."

Becky raised her glass and added, "I'd like to add my hope that the next four years are more peaceful than the last."

Renee joined them and added, "To freedom."

Renee joined them and added, "To freedom."

That evening, after Renee and André and the little ones had returned to their own cabin, Dan carved two pegs and inserted them in the chinking above the fireplace. He placed the Sharp's on them and turned to answer Becky's unspoken "why?"

"I think it needs a resting place. I don't think I will be needing it except for hunting anymore."

Becky reached out to him with both hands. "Oh, I hope so. What of all that talk about Southern secession if Lincoln is elected?"

He reached out and encircled her waist. "Lincoln won't even be nominated. He is an able speaker, but Seward is better known. He'll be the Republican nominee, and the Democrats will nominate Steven Douglas. Douglas will win the election, and things will go on as before."

He pulled her close and led her toward the bedroom.

"Now let's take up that kissing where we left off this morning."

Afterword:

Facts and timeframe are as accurate as I can make them. The Doyle family, Martin White, Brockett, Pate, Nathan Stone and his daughter Lydia, John Armstrong and his sister, Sarah, and the Scales family, Colonel Henry Titus, who actually did not go straight to Florida on leaving Kansas but did found Titusville, Florida, are all real people as are the better known characters such as James Lane, John Brown, Fredrick Douglass, Harriet Tubman, Major Buford, Henry Clay Pate, James Montgomery, Charles Jennison, James Butler Hickok, better known by his later nickname Wild Bill Hickok, JEB Stuart, Jo Shelby, Colonel Sumner and most of the military officers mentioned. The battle dates and events are as accurate as I can make them. The yell heard at Hickory Point is credited with being the early version of the famous Rebel Yell.

While not being privy to all their private conversations, I tried to closely fit conversations to what I learned of their characters from numerous hours of research both online and in printed sources. Since the Underground Railroad was, of necessity, shrouded in secrecy, the stationmasters are real people who were believed to have taken part in aiding escaped slaves to freedom, but actual records are hard to locate.

The shooting by Lane of his neighbor, Giaus Jenkins, is a true event. You will read more of the real life lawyer who defended Lane, Thomas Ewing, in the second book of this series, *Under A Black Flag*.

It wasn't until the last year of his life that Brown grew his famous beard - he probably stopped shaving in late fall of 1857. By the spring of the following year, he had a full beard. Contemporary drawings of Brown made when he was arrested show that his beard had been either been trimmed close or shaved off altogether. (*http://www. adirondackalmanack.com/2009/11/last-days-of-john-brown-famous-beard.html*)

Kansas Territory went through ten acting governors and submitted four different constitutions between 1854 and 1860 before achieving statehood in January 1861.

A preview of *Under A Black Flag* to be released in 2011

Prologue
November 1860—Pottawattamie Creek, Kansas Territory

Dan and Andre were looking over their flourishing winter wheat crop. Dan's dogs, Mason and Dixon, frolicked nearby. Unless someone pointed out that the two men were half-brothers, no one would guess, considering Andre's African heritage was clearly stamped on his features even though he was just a few shades darker than Dan. Andre's ebony hair had a lot of curl whereas Dan's wavy light brown hair had glints of blond streaked through it by the Kansas sun. Both men were tall and slim with broad shoulders.

The men who came charging out of the brush certainly didn't see them as brothers. The leader of the pack was a short man with a Cossack cap on his head and the uniform of Charles Jennison's 7th Kansas Cavalry. Every Southerner dreaded a visit from the Redlegs, so called because of the red gaiters on their legs. Their leader, Charles Jennison, was a bandy little man who patrolled the area near the Missouri border and made a practice of robbing and killing anyone with any Southern connection.

They had gotten the soubrette when one of their members, Pat Devlin, also referred to as "Pat with a devil in him," was seen entering a Kansas border village with a horse so loaded down with loot it was almost hidden from view. Asked what he had been up to, Pat replied he'd been out "jayhawking." When asked what that term meant, Devlin stated, "I have been foraging off the enemy and while riding home on me beast, I bethought me of the bird we have in Ireland, we call the jayhawk, which takes delight in worryin' its prey before devouring it, and I thought 'jayhawking' a good name for the business I was in meself."

A local wag noted, "They gave themselves up to plundering, robbing and stealing from everybody and anybody. They pretended to be Free-State men – called themselves so – but any man who had a little property was a Pro-Slavery man in their eyes, and 'all horses were Pro-Slavery.'"

Dan recognized them instantly and knew there was going to be a problem. He had left his rifle in the cabin with his wife, Becky. She knew how to use it, but there were too many of these desperados even if he, Becky, Andre and Andre's wife, Renee, had been armed and ready. At least Renee, who was a runaway slave, was relatively safe from this band since they proclaimed themselves Free-State men out to stamp out slavery and run any Southerners out of Kansas. Those they did not run out, they killed. Just recently, little Doc Jennison and his band had hanged an old man named Samuel Scott in his own yard. They had also hanged another man, Russ Hines. Their latest outrage had been to break into L.D. Moore's home during the night and shoot him as he slept in his bed. Moore had been a member of a vigilante group sworn to stop the widespread horse theft in the area.

When Moore and his fellow vigilantes had recently lynched a horse thief, who rode with Jennison, the Redleg commander decided to pay Moore a visit in the dead of night and teach him a lesson. After killing Moore, Jennison had ridden to the home of Mr. Hudson, whose wife was related to Moore. Jennison coolly informed Mrs. Hudson of what he had done and demanded she provide breakfast for his party.

Dan felt his best chance was not to anger Jennison. The man had proven he had a very short fuse. Gritting his teeth, Dan tried for a civil tone. "You gentlemen looking for someone?'

Jennison reined his horse in so he looked down on Dan and Andre. He spat a stream of yellow tobacco. "Yeah, I sure am. I'm hunting down any slave-holding Southerons." He shot a glance toward Andre. "You, boy. You're free now. Ain't no need for you to be hoeing this lowlife's field. Git."

Andre didn't move. "We're partners. It's my field too."

Jennison snickered. He addressed the man riding next to him. "Funny partner for a Negro to have, huh, Marshall?"

His eyes had never left Dan. "What you doing in Kansas? It's a free territory and gonna be a free state soon. No place for the likes of you."

Dan stared back at the little captain. "This is my claim. I'm neutral in this fight. Andre is not a slave; he is a free man. I freed him before I came to Kansas."

"Neutral?" Jennison laughed. "Neutrality is impossible; if you are patriots, you must fight; if your are traitors, you will be punished. Traitors will everywhere be treated as outlaws; enemies of God and man, too base to hold any description of property, and having no rights which loyal men are bound to respect. You have no right to this claim or any Kansas land."

The man Jennison had addressed as Marshall sneered. "Neutral? I think you are just another stinking traitor." He looked toward his commander. "Shall I take him for trial or just shoot him here?"

Jennison looked over the claim to the simple cabin. "Naw, he doesn't seem to be a big problem or have lots of valuables. Just fire his cabin and wheat crop." He returned his attention to Dan. "We're just giving you a warning this time. We'll be back within a month to be sure you understood that your kind aren't welcome in Kansas. Got it?"

Jennison wheeled his horse and joined his men who were lighting torches and setting the fields aflame. "If you've got a woman and any young'uns in that cabin, you better get them out unless you want them cooked to a crisp."

Jamison's lieutenant, Marshall, echoed, "Yeah and then head for the woods. If"n I see you trying to stop us, you could get shot accidentally like. Understand?"

The only other time Dan had felt this helpless was when he was a prisoner of John Brown after the Battle of Black Jack. He looked at Andre who nodded his understanding of the hopelessness of attempting to resist. "Let's do as the *gentleman* says," Andre urged.

The two of them hurried over to the cabin to get Becky to safety. She was on the porch, holding his Sharpe's rifle, Little Thunder, as Dan had assumed. She, too, had realized that they could not successfully stop the Redlegs and if they resisted things could get much worse. Becky handed Dan the gun and fell into his arms. "I feel so helpless. They are burning our crops, and there is nothing we can do," she moaned.

Dan held her close for a moment then released her. "It's going to get worse. They plan to fire the cabin. Go to Andre's cabin. Warn Renee. You two take the children and stay in the woods until either Andre or I come for you."

Becky took one last look at their flaming wheat field. She rushed to the bedroom to grab a handful of precious belongings and ducked out the door and ran toward Andre's cabin, Mason and Dixon right behind her. Dan waited just long enough to be sure no one was following Becky. He turned to Andre. "Let's gather up all the blankets and then hide behind the barn. We'll need to hide the horses. No way around it, they are going to steal the rest of the stock, but if they don't fire the barn, we can wet the blankets in the horse trough and maybe salvage some of the cabin after those dammed Redlegs leave."

Dan put action to words and scooped blankets over his rifle. Andre grabbed the others, and they headed for the barn.

Andre peered out from a corner. "Danged if I wouldn't love to put a few bullets in those thieving bastards.

Dan had just returned from tying their horses in the woods far out of view of the Jayhawkers. He had acquired Chieftain, his palomino, when Becky rescued him from a sure hanging by Jim Lane, one of the Free-State leaders, in Lawrence. Andre had picked up his spirited stallion, Silver, during one of Andre's Underground Railroad trips.

Andre said little about that subject to protect Dan, but Dan was aware his half-brother acted as a conductor to help runaway slaves. It had begun after Andre had helped a group of fugitive slaves. Andre's wife, Renee, had been a member of that group but unable to continue to freedom due to the severe beatings she had suffered at the hands of a former mistress. Dan wished him well as he too now disapproved of slavery.

They watched in helpless fury as the outlaws turned from the now blazing wheat fields to the little cabin. Before firing it, several of the Redlegs dismounted and entered. They began bundling items from the house on the porch in bags. Obviously they planned to get all the valuables before they burned the cabin.

Dan let out a long hissing breath. "Damn. I hope Becky was wearing her scrimshaw combs. They are the only thing she was able to take when she rescued me from Lane. They were made by her grandfather for her when she was a child, and they mean so much to her."

The Jayhawkers rapaciousness proved their undoing. As the pile on the porch mounted, the sound of many galloping hoofbeats approaching caused them to throw themselves into their saddles with what they had already stolen and make a fast escape. Jennison himself leading the troop.

Dan and Andre raced toward the porch with their wet blankets and began beating the flames out. Instants later, a detachment of federal soldiers reined in and proceeded to help. The fire was put out quickly with little damage. It had not had time to catch well, unlike the one that had almost decimated the wheat field.

Andre nodded his thanks to the troop and went over to meet Becky and Renee who, with little Dawn and Pill, his and Renee's daughter and son, were just peering out from the edge of the woods. Dan turned to the young captain. "Daniel Fitzgerald, sir. Thank you for your timely arrival."

The soldier answered, "Captain Walker of the U. S. army. I'm part of the two detachments of cavalry from Fort Riley. We were called in by Acting Governor Beebe to try and put a stop to just this sort of thing."

The two men shook hands."Well, you were certainly a welcome sight here," Dan said

"Jennison and his bunch have already frightened away over five hundred settlers. Some have taken shelter in Fort Scott, and most have left for parts unknown."

Becky and Renee, accompanied by André, added their thanks to Dan's. The two women began sorting through the broken items strewn across the porch. Becky's red-gold hair was in disarray, and a black smudge marred her freckled face. Her blue eyes were filled with tears. Renee's emerald eyes misted in sympathy.

"The Jayhawkers said they will be back to be sure we leave the territory." Dan cast a worried glance at his wife. She was of sturdy New England stock, but there was a limit to what a person could stand.

"You can be sure they will, sir," Walker replied. "They usually have operated in Linn and Bourbon counties, but they sometimes branch into adjoining counties like Franklin."

"Can't you arrest them or at least the leaders, Lane, Jennison and Montgomery?" Dan asked.

The captain shook his head. "They are too well protected and have too many men on their side. Lane is not openly involved but everyone knows he sanctions this sort of thing. He is one of the most powerful men in Kansas Territory. The best we can do is try and patrol mostly in Linn and Bourbon counties. We just happened to be riding nearby and saw the smoke."

"It's a sad state when a territory, soon to be a state, can't protect its own citizens," Dan commented.

Walker replied. "I agree, sir. However, this conflict had been going on almost since the territory was opened and doesn't seem like statehood will end it. If you feel unsafe here, you and your families are welcome to shelter at Fort Scott."

Dan shook his head. "And then what? Come back to a burned cabin and wasted fields. No thanks. I reckon Kansas will never welcome Southerners. It's time my family and I pull up and move where we are more welcome."

Later that evening, Dan and Andre gathered some of the bedding and walked over to Andre's cabin where Becky waited along with Renee. They had assessed the damage to the wheat crop. It was almost totally wiped out. The cabin had suffered only minor damage. Some foodstuffs and a few items from the living room and kitchen had been taken. The canned foods were all broken and scattered around the kitchen. It could easily be fixed and replaced. What could not be as easily repaired was Dan's self esteem. He had tried to make Kansas safe for his family and build a life away from his father's plantation in Louisiana. He had tried to be a man and stand on his own two feet. He felt a miserable failure. This time he had been too outnumbered to even fight back. When the two families were seated around the new large dining table Andre had recently built to replace the stump used previously, Dan spoke up. "I've come to a decision. Not an easy one by any means. I think it is time to leave Kansas and move across the border to Missouri. Becky, it's your life too, if you don't want to move, we'll keep trying here."

Becky hesitated. "What about Andre and Renee and the kids?"

Dan knew Becky loved his brother's children all the more deeply since she and Dan had none of their own. "Andre, you know you and your family are welcome to join us if you could."

The unsaid words were "but I know you can't." Renee was a fugitive slave. In Kansas, soon to be a free state, she was relatively safe. In Missouri, a slave state, she would quickly be apprehended and returned to her owner. Worse, the children, Dawn Rebecca, almost four, and Pilgrim Daniel, about to celebrate his second birthday this month, would also be enslaved. Andre nodded in affirmation of what didn't need to be said. "We all know that we can't move. Dan, you can take all of what we have in the bank. You'll need at least that to buy any land there at all."

"Thanks, Andre, but I can't do that. I just need my share, and I don't even feel I should take that since it is my fault those Redlegs burned the wheat."

Andre snorted. "Your fault my foot, Danny Boy. Those murdering scum are to blame. No one else."

Renee nodded her agreement. Becky sat silently with tears flowing down her cheeks. Renee reached over and hugged her. "You can always come visit. If you settle in Cass County or one of the border counties, it's not too far."

Becky spoke through her tears. "I know we can't seem to find any peace here. I know you've made a right choice. But it's hard. So very hard."

About the Author:

Along with being the author of several books, Kathleen is also a successful travel writer/photographer who has been published in numerous publications including *Woodall's Publications, Family Motor Coaching, Amateur Chef, Georgia Magazine, Georgia Backroads, London, England's Country Music People* and others. She currently publishes her own online travel magazine, *American Roads* (www.americanroads.net).

Kathleen has worked as a reporter for a local paper and had her own TV show on a local station at one time. She has been a speaker or workshop presenter at places such as Rotary Club, Lions, Young Harris College, Flagler County Continuing Education and other venues. She has appeared on television shows such as "Art With A Capital A" at WGNM TV and a Turner Blue Ribbon Special. History has always been one of her favoriet subjects. She resides in Eustis, Florida along with more cats than she wants to mention.

Other books by Kathleen Walls:

Finding Florida's Phantoms: The best haunted spots in Florida
Last Step. A story of drugs, love and murder set in Jacksonville, Florida
Man Hunt-The Eric Rudolph Story. A close-up look at an American terrorist.
Kudzu: A tale of love and betrayal-past and present-in the North Georgia Mountains.
Tax Sale Tactics: Learn how to buy property at bargain prices at tax sales.
Sarah: A Confederate Girl's Diary. An actual Civil War diary of a young woman in Baton Rouge with a forward by Kathleen.
The Wild About Florida series with Martin Walls
Please visit her web site, www.katywalls.com.
You can email her at katyrw@hotmail.com.